SHAY'S SHIFT

Mountain Men of Montana 1

Jane Jamison

MENAGE EVERLASTING

Siren Publishing, Inc.
www.SirenPublishing.com

A SIREN PUBLISHING BOOK
IMPRINT: Ménage Everlasting

SHAY'S SHIFTERS
Copyright © 2013 by Jane Jamison

ISBN: 978-1-62242-352-1

First Printing: January 2013

Cover design by Les Byerley
All art and logo copyright © 2013 by Siren Publishing, Inc.

Printed in the U.S.A.

PUBLISHER
Siren Publishing, Inc.
www.SirenPublishing.com

SHAY'S SHIFTERS

Mountain Men of Montana 1

JANE JAMISON
Copyright © 2013

Chapter One

Shaylyn Mathews knocked on the front door of her friend's home. The quick trip from California to Montana and then up the treacherous road that wound around the mountain to Willa Schutte's cabin had left her dazed and weary. But she'd had no choice. After getting Willa's frantic, garbled cell phone message begging her to come, she'd rushed to her aide. Her friend had needed her, and that's all she'd needed to know.

Everything outside the home appeared peaceful. Willa's SUV as well as Bill's Jeep sat in the driveway. Holiday lights were strung along the porch railing as they were for most of the year. She smiled, remembering the discussions she'd had trying to convince Bill to take them down after the holiday season.

She knocked again and wondered if she should see if they were around the back of the home. If Willa and Bill were outside, they might not hear her knocking. For the hundredth time, she wondered why Willa had begged her to come. It wasn't like her friend to act that way.

She was about to head toward the back when Willa, her mousy brown hair clinging to her face, cracked open the door. Her glassy eyes looked at Shay as though she didn't recognize her. She was unkempt, dressed in a soiled nightgown, and, judging from the grime on her skin as well as the body odor, Shay assumed that her friend hadn't bathed recently.

"Willa, are you all right? Can I come in?"

Her friend's gaze darted around the yard, making Shay look again to see if she'd overlooked something. But she couldn't find anything out of the ordinary. Or at least in terms of how it had looked the last time she'd visited.

"Sweetie, let me in." She kept her voice low, her tone soft. "You have to let me inside, okay?"

Willa shook her head. "No. Go away."

"But you told me to come."

"Go away." For a second, she saw her friend in the glassy eyes sunken in the haggard-looking face. "Please, Shay."

What had happened to her? Was she pleading for her to leave or to help her? She was shocked when Willa made a small cry and slammed the door.

What the hell?

The small knot in her stomach that had started with the phone call tightened. If she didn't get to the bottom of things soon, it would grow to softball size.

"Willa, what's wrong? Bill? Are you there, Bill? Will one of you please open the door?"

After several attempts to get them to open the door, Shay couldn't stand it any longer. "I'm coming inside." She turned the doorknob and was surprised to find it unlocked.

Pushing the door wide, she stepped over the threshold of what she'd once declared the tidiest home in America and into a nightmare.

The house looked like a hurricane had whipped its mighty tail around the interior. Furniture lay strewn and broken everywhere, along with leftover food and broken dishes. Torn curtains clung to their rods by strips of cloth. In their place, aluminum foil was layered over the windows, blocking the sun's rays and giving off a shiny, eerie glow.

Neither Willa nor Bill was in sight. "Willa? Where are you?"

Red slashes on the walls brought her attention away from the chaos of the room. At first, she didn't understand that the scribbles were words. But as she continued to stare at them, she finally made out the scrawled messages.

Stay away

Leave us alone

Evil

Die Die Die Die

A crash to her left startled her and she let out a yelp, pivoting quickly to face the dining room that led into the adjoining kitchen. Shards of a broken plate lay at Willa's feet. Blood trickled down the front of her legs and spread outward from cuts on the tops of her feet.

"Shit, sweetie." She moved toward her friend then stopped as Willa shuffled away from her, putting the table between them.

Oh, my God. She's terrified of me. But why? I have to help her, but how?

She edged around the table, but Willa kept moving, dodging first one way then the other. Shay faked her out, caught her, and latched on to her arm. Willa struggled a moment, then dropped her chin and stared at the floor.

She led her into the living room and forced her to sit on the sofa next to her. A ragged, nasty scratch ran down her arm, but at least it didn't look like it was infected. She pulled off the scarf she wore and dotted the wounds on her friend's legs and feet.

"Willa, please tell me what's wrong." Shay took another quick look around, still not believing her eyes. Had they suffered a home invasion? Had they contracted a horrible disease? Even if the latter was true, she still couldn't help but take her friend's hands.

Willa shook her head before lifting it to give her another blank stare. "I don't know."

She breathed a sigh of relief. At least Willa seemed more coherent now.

"Did someone hurt you?" When Willa didn't answer, she readied herself for the worst possible answer to her next question. "Is Bill okay? Is he here?"

With the mention of her husband's name, Willa glanced toward the hallway that led to the large master suite. "He's in bed."

She'd check on Bill once she was sure Willa was all right. "What happened to the house? To you?"

Again, Willa shook her head. "I'm not sure. The last thing I remember is walking in the woods with Bill."

"Did something happen in the woods?"

The diminutive woman squeezed Shay's hands so hard that she had to bite back a cry. Willa let out a fearful and horrifying whine.

"Some *thing* jumped us. Bill cried out, and when I turned toward him…" She yanked her hands away and dug her fingers into her hair. "Nooo. I don't want to think about it."

A knot closed around Shay's heart. Despite her size, Willa was a strong, independent woman. She was a woman who had faced hardships in her life and had come out on top. Whatever had happened had to be more than Shay could imagine and obviously more than Willa could handle.

She pulled her friend into her arms then stroked her hair, trying to soothe the agonized woman. "It's okay. I'm here now. Nothing's going to hurt you. I promise everything's going to be fine."

Willa's thin arms wrapped around her and hugged her, clinging to Shay like a lifeline. "I can't remember what it looked like. I can't. I can't. I can't."

"Shh. You don't have to."

They sat on the sofa for several minutes. Shay comforted her as best she could, saying reassuring words like she would to a frightened child who'd screamed in the middle of the night about monsters in the closet.

At last, Willa calmed down enough to turn her loose. Shay stood and, still gripping her hand, took Willa along with her. Hoping she'd find Bill alive, Shay pulled Willa down the hall and into the master bedroom.

Bill lay on the bed, his chest heaving as he struggled to breathe. She pried Willa's hand from hers and rushed to his side. His eyes were closed, and his shirt and hair were soaked with sweat and plastered against his skin. Three deep scratches ran down his cheek. The jeans he wore looked like they were two sizes too large, and yet she knew Bill would never wear baggy clothes. Had he lost so much weight in the months since she'd last seen him?

"Bill, can you open your eyes? It's Shay Mathews."

She held her breath, waiting for a response, a reaction, even the twitch of a finger, but received none. Seeing Willa in her horrible condition was bad enough, but seeing strong, virile Bill sent a chill down her spine. Whatever had happened wasn't anything she could solve. She pulled out her phone and dialed 9-1-1.

The emergency operator answered on the second ring. Shay took a second to thank her lucky stars since she knew cell phone reception was hit-and-miss in the mountains. But at least it had hit this time.

"I need an ambulance at 529 Amber Lane. Yes, it's up in the mountains. It's a right turn off Ridge Road. Can you please hurry? My friends are very ill. No, I don't know what's wrong with them. Just hurry."

The operator suggested she stay on the line, so she held on to the phone and turned back to find Willa standing in front of the large ceiling-to-floor picture window overlooking the backyard and the forest beyond. Willa's back was ramrod straight, and, for one wonderful moment, she thought her friend had snapped out of whatever awful thing possessed her.

"Hold on, Willa. Help's coming."

She heard the operator's voice and brought the phone back to her ear. "Yeah. I'm still here. But I need to do more than wait. Yes, I'll hang on."

She pulled the bedspread rumpled at Bill's feet up to his chin then laid her palm against his clammy cheek.

Bill had swept Willa off her feet two years earlier, and although Shay had never liked him much, she'd seen how happy he'd made her friend. For that reason alone, she cared about him.

She brought the phone back to her ear. "I don't know what happened. Their names are Bill and Willa Schutte. I think they're ill, but I'm not sure. They may have had an intruder in the home. What? No, there's no one else here." At least she didn't think so. Maybe she should've checked before assuming that.

She walked over to Willa's side, putting the phone against her chest. "Sweetie, is anyone else in the house? Did someone break in and do this to you?" But even if an intruder had broken in, would that explain Willa's odd behavior?

Willa didn't answer. Instead, she placed a hand against the windowpane. A tear slid down her cheek. "I used to love it here."

"You'll love it again. You'll get past this. I know you will. And when you do, you'll love it again."

The forest outside was as beautiful as she remembered. The blanket of snow made the peaceful scene surreal, giving it a fairy-tale quality that a snowfall in a city could never match.

She sighed and wondered if her hometown of Passion, Colorado, had gotten its first big snowfall yet. She'd told her friend Tatum Griffin that she was coming home soon to meet the three Shelton men she lived with. After taking several months exploring California for a new home, she'd given up and had decided to return to Passion and her roots. Willa's call, however, had delayed her trip, or she would've been home by now.

"What are you looking at?"

Willa didn't answer immediately, and when she did, her voice changed, growing dark and ominous. "The woods are so beautiful."

How can she say it's beautiful yet sound so grave? Maybe she's not thinking straight yet. Please let help come soon.

"Yeah. It's pretty cool out here, especially when it snows."

"Don't let it fool you. The blackness hides within it."

Shay couldn't help but shiver. When had the perpetually effervescent Willa ever sounded so grim? "What do you mean?"

Willa turned to her, her usually dancing eyes solemn and sad. "Be careful. Don't let it get you."

It? "Don't let what get me?"

Bill moaned, turning both of them toward him. Willa scurried over to the bed, climbed on top of it, and molded her body to his.

Shay moved toward the door, telling herself that she needed to watch for the paramedics. Yet as soon as she stepped outside the bedroom and closed the door behind her, she couldn't hide from the fact that she'd needed to get away from her friends. It was almost as though they contained the darkness Willa spoke of and could somehow infect her.

* * * *

Shay had followed her friends to the local hospital and had given the doctors as much information as she could. Uncomfortable staying at her friend's home while they weren't there, she'd rented a room at a small family-run motel a few miles down the road.

The next day, she went back to Willa's home and changed the bedding, washing it in hot water then deciding at the last moment to throw it in the trash and replace it with different bedding. She scoured the kitchen as well as the three bathrooms and sprayed disinfectant everywhere. After hauling the broken furniture to the backyard, she made a list of items they'd need to replace. But she'd let Willa and Bill do that part if and when they wanted to. Yet, even after putting the home in order, she sensed that the horror that had befallen her friends didn't reside in the house. Instead, she found herself gazing at the woods, searching as hard as she could for…something.

She returned to the hospital the second night, hoping for good news, but the doctors still didn't understand what was wrong. In place of a real answer, they assured Shay that they'd continue to do the best they could. Shay contacted their families and, at their insistence, agreed to stay on until they could arrive the next day.

On the third day, an hour before Willa's brother and Bill's sister arrived, Willa and Bill suddenly awakened as though from a bad dream. They even seemed like their old selves.

Except for the fact that they couldn't remember what had happened.

Shay hugged her friends good-bye and, leaving them to their relieved relatives, hurried back to the motel. Although a part of her wanted to stay until they were discharged from the hospital, another part of her wanted nothing more than to get away. She'd explained as much to her friends, who had thanked her and had assured her that they were fine.

Shay punched the buttons on her phone. The past grueling days were over, and she couldn't wait to get home to Passion.

"Hello? Is that you, you skinny bitch?"

As it usually did whenever she spoke to Tatum, a smile formed on her face. She could envision her friend's long brown hair, hazel eyes, and the freckles that skimmed over the bridge of her nose. Yet, even though she hadn't seen her friend for months, she could sense that Tatum had changed. The shy girl with the large glasses and oversized clothes was gone. Since meeting the three Shelton brothers, Tatum had transformed, abruptly changing into a confident, sexy young woman. She didn't have to see her friend to know it was true. She could hear it in her voice.

"Yeah, it's me. The Bitch of the West. Although skinny I'm not."

"Bitch in name only. Shay, where the hell are you anyway? I expected you back home by now. Or did you find a hot California surfer dude to hook up with?"

She couldn't blame her friend for jumping to that assumption. If she'd found a hot surfer dude, she wouldn't have hesitated to stay on to enjoy both him and the beach. As far as Shay was concerned, life was for fun, and she wasn't going to miss a single second. Although she knew she wasn't what most people would call beautiful, she could hold her own with men. In fact, she was sure that most of them preferred a woman with curves instead of the flat-chested, bony bitches the advertising world inflicted on society. She had generous breasts and was damn proud of it, flaunting her "girls" with low-cut tops every time she got the chance. Her face wasn't classically attractive with her wide forehead and her round face, but she thought she looked intelligent and yet still approachable, forming a combination that most men liked.

Shay had led a charmed life. The only daughter of doting, wealthy parents, she'd had everything she'd ever wanted. If she lived two lifetimes, she couldn't spend all the money in her trust fund. Yet, according to everyone who knew her, she'd remained unspoiled, caring, and giving. And ready to play on the wild side of life as often as she could.

She'd tried to find a place to settle in during her long trek around California, but no place had ever come close to feeling like home. How she'd ever thought she could find a better place to live than Passion, Colorado, she'd never know. She missed the artsy, eclectic community where billionaires like her parents mixed easily with starving artists and the tourists who flocked to the small town in the summer months. Passion had its share of the eccentric, too, and there were even rumors that supernatural beings such as werewolves and vampires lived in and around the town. She'd seen a few things in her life to make her think that the rumors might be true.

"Shay, are you there?"

"Yeah, I'm still here. But no such luck about the man thing. I, um, took a detour."

"A detour? Where to?"

"To a friend's house." She'd tell Tatum what happened at Willa's home, but not over the phone. Some things needed to be told in person. "But I'm leaving today. I should get to Passion in a couple of days."

"You mean unless another detour pops up."

Shay laughed for the first time since she'd arrived at Willa's. "Well, you know what I always say. If opportunity knocks, open the damn door."

"Yeah, I know. Okay, then. But I expect you to call me the minute you get back into town."

"I promise. Make sure those three men of yours are ready for an interrogation. If I think they're good enough for you, I might let you keep them."

Tatum's laugh was bright and cheery, sending Shay the warmth she needed. "Girl, no one's taking my men away from me. Not even you."

"Okay, now I've really got to meet them. They must be super special."

"You don't know the half of it. Drive carefully and be safe."

"Got it. Check you soon, Tee." She punched the off button and snatched up her suitcase. "I can't wait to get the hell out of here."

She swung by the front desk, dropped off the key, then hurried to her car.

Shay scraped off the mound of snow that had accumulated on her hood and windshield as she let her Porsche warm up. The snow had started coming down in large, white flakes, adding to the inch of wet stuff already making the road hazardous to drive. She'd never liked driving in less than favorable conditions, and each trip she'd made between Willa's home, the hospital, and her motel had shaken her nerves. She hated winding around the hillside with the sharp drop off the side only a half foot from the edge of her wheels, but at least she'd only have to do it once more. However, with the extra inches of powder added, the drive down would be even harder.

She checked the position of the sun heading toward the western horizon then looked at her phone for the time. Leaving in midafternoon gave her plenty of cushion to make it down the mountain before nightfall set in.

Or at least that's what she hoped.

She slipped into the driver's side and cranked up the heater. Not for the first time, she wished she'd left her car in a city at the base of the mountain range and rented a pickup or Jeep with snow chains for the trip to Willa's. But she'd wanted to get to her friend as fast as possible.

"I can do this. All I have to do is take it slow and easy." She'd managed other roads during storms and less than desirable conditions, and she'd manage this one, too. Pulling away from the motel, she glanced back once and sent good thoughts to her friends still recuperating in the hospital.

Ten minutes later, she'd relaxed enough to sing along with the Pink CD she'd popped into the player. The edge of the mountainside was still too close for comfort, but she kept her gaze on the road ahead and away from the terrifying free fall. Yet no matter how she tried, she couldn't shake Willa's ominous warning.

What had she meant? What was the blackness in the woods? For a moment, she was thankful that the road was flanked on one side by the rocky cliff and on the other by the steep drop over the side. No forest meant no blackness, right?

She shrugged off the tension tightening her shoulders and focused on what she'd do once she made it home to Passion. First, she'd check in with friends, especially Tatum. She was dying to meet the men Tee had fallen in love with in such a short time.

Was it love at first sight? She scoffed. She'd never believed in that kind of thing. How could she when she'd never fallen in love at all? Love was a two-sided sword. One day it would bring happiness, and, in the next, it could bring despair and heartache. She had no desire to leave her fun-loving life, free to roam wherever and whenever she wanted.

She slowed down to maneuver around a curve and noticed that

she'd reached the part of the road that was bordered on one side by the statuesque trees. Again, she thought of Willa's words then shoved them out of her mind. Why focus on such dreariness when all was right with the world again?

She let out a sigh then reached over to flip through the stack of CDs on the passenger seat. Grabbing another disc, she punched the player's eject button, snatched Pink out of the player, and slipped the new one in.

She glanced up, and all hell broke loose.

Like a bear standing on its hind legs, a dark shape stood in the middle of the road, its front legs bent like a dog begging for a bone. A thin neck led to an oval-shaped head and large, elongated red eyes glowed in a face that seemed more alien than human. Flashing long, deadly fangs, the thing leapt out from in front of the car to disappear into the woods.

Shay let out a scream and stomped on the brake, sending the car into a tailspin. She clutched the steering wheel then turned into the spin, but by then the vehicle was a bullet already flying toward its destination. Blurred images of the edge of the cliff, then the trees, then the cliff again whirled by her until finally coming to rest on the trees. The Porsche struck a tree dead-on, throwing her body back then forward.

Pain seared through her forehead. A warm substance slimed its way down, over her eyebrow and onto her eyelid. She kept her eyes shut, letting the shudder ricocheting through her body come to its final destination at the bottom of her feet. The ache in her head intensified when she opened her eyes.

Snowflakes drifted toward the ground as she stared through her side window and into the trees. Quiet as the dead, the world around her continued, oblivious to her predicament. She moaned, searching outward with her hands until she finally gripped the steering wheel. She pushed backward until her shoulders rested against the back of her seat. The vision in her right eye blurred as blood dripped into it.

What the hell happened?

She needed to know, wanted to know, but couldn't bring herself to move. Moving meant pain, and she'd had enough of that. Instead of thinking, she concentrated on her breathing, pulling in air through her nose then letting it out her mouth. And still the snow fell.

She couldn't have said how long she sat in the same position, staring straight ahead, making no movement aside from the rise and fall of her chest. As though viewing the world through binoculars from a faraway place, she watched as the dusting of snow on her hood grew higher. Thought finally broke through the haze, forcing her back into the world around her.

What was that thing I saw? Is it still here?

She dragged in a deep breath, prepared herself for the pain, then turned her head. Agony struck her, singeing up from the middle of her forehead to travel over her head and down her neck.

Look.

She listened to the inner voice compelling her to ignore everything, every pain, every ache to concentrate on what she could see. Yet she saw only the beauty of the snowbound forest.

Look the other way.

Again, she pushed away the torment pounding in her head and turned to scan the other side. And again, she saw nothing but the woods.

Maybe I scared it away.

She was almost certain she hadn't hit it. Too bad she couldn't say the same thing about the tree. From the way the hood of the vehicle was bent upward toward the windshield she assumed it was useless to try to start the car, but she did it anyway. As she'd expected, the car was dead.

Groaning, she pulled the lever and opened the door. If she'd hit it, she wanted to know. Pivoting to get out, she put her feet on the ground, sinking her boots into a half foot of snow.

Fighting against a sudden rush of nausea, she took hold of the car door and yanked her body into a standing position. She cried out as her knees gave in and she crumpled to the ground.

She lay on the ground, the cold and wetness seeping into her. Sunlight filtered through the trees above her, entrancing her into staying where she was. Would someone come along and find her? It was unlikely considering she hadn't seen a car from the moment she'd left the motel.

Get moving. If you lie here, you're going to freeze to death once night comes.

Yelping at the pain her movements inflicted, she rolled over onto her stomach then pushed her body into a sitting position. She shook her head, ridding her face of the snow. The world spun around her to create a kaleidoscope of dark browns mixed with brilliant white.

My phone.

She twisted around slowly, painstakingly, to search the car. Her phone rested on the floor mat, so close, and yet the distance seemed insurmountable. Still, she tried, once again bringing a stabbing flash of pain. Against her will, her tears broke free, but she managed a shout of victory as her fingertips touched her cell phone.

Call for help.

Idly, she wondered if calling 9-1-1 twice in less than a week was a new record.

She clasped her phone and brought it in front of her face. Wiping away the blood that had settled on her eyelid, she squinted at the phone and tried to make out the screen. But her eyes wouldn't focus enough for her to see the icons. Instead, she gambled, pressing what she hoped was the On button. Swiping her finger across the screen, she heard the familiar sound of her cell unlocking, and she smiled, for the first time feeling a spark of hope.

She looked harder, willing her eyes to see the phone icon. When at last her vision grew clearer, she punched it and saw the display change into the large numbers of the keypad. She punched in 9-1-1 and put the receiver to her ear.

Nothing. No dial tone. No sound at all. She bit her lower lip and forced herself to stay calm.

I'm going to get out of this. Think. Don't let your emotions take over.

She swallowed and tried going through the steps again. Still no sound. Fear trickled into her, but she pushed it back again, determined not to give in. Shoving the phone into the pocket of her jacket, she grabbed the door with one hand and flattened her other palm against the side of the car. Gritting back a cry, she stood up and tested her legs.

Okay. I'm still on my feet. That's good. I can find my own help.

She glanced around and saw the tracks her car had made in the road as it had spun around and into the forest. She'd gotten lucky that her car hadn't careened off the side of the mountain.

Gathering her wits, she decided that she had four choices. She could stay inside the car and wait for help to come. But she wasn't the type to wait, and who knew how long it would be before someone came along.

She could walk back to the motel. She wasn't sure how long it would take, but at least once there she'd get dry and warm. Scanning the road back the way she'd come, she weighed her chances of walking up the icy road with its steep incline. She doubted she could make it without losing her footing and either breaking a bone or slipping off the edge and plummeting to her death.

Should she start walking downhill? But going downhill was as slippery as going uphill, and she knew it would take her hours before she'd make it to the first rest stop that had a gas station.

She turned and faced the woods. Could she make it very far in the forest? Once she'd taken that route, she'd have little chance that anyone would find her. Not that anyone was looking. Willa and Bill would assume she'd made it off the mountain and wouldn't check on her. Only Tatum knew she was headed home, and if she didn't show up in two days, Tee would simply assume that she'd taken another detour. Weeks would have to pass before Tee grew worried enough to raise an alarm.

She rubbed her arms, fighting against the chill creeping into her bones, and made her choice. At least if she made it downhill, she had a chance of running into someone. She'd just have to keep moving and hope that would keep her warm enough until she found help.

Shay took a step toward the road then stopped at the crashing sound that came from directly behind her. Whirling around, she stared, alarm clogging her throat.

Could it be the Thing I saw on the road?

A small fawn broke through the trees and slammed to a stop. Its huge black eyes fixed on her, looking as stunned as she felt. The fawn's light brown coat was dotted with dark spots. It was a vision of wilderness beauty against the pristine backdrop of the snow-covered trees.

A giggle escaped as relief swamped her. *The Thing? Drama queen much? What next? The creature from* Alien? *Get a grip, girl.*

A fawn was better than confronting the Thing in the road. She smiled and forgot about the pain in her forehead for the first time since running into the trees.

But her joy was short lived as a dark movement to the right and back of the fawn caught her attention. Was that the Thing? Or something even worse?

A vision of the glowing eyes and the long fangs froze her. Warning bells clanged in her head to get back into the car, and yet she stayed where she was. After everything that had happened, after everything she'd seen and done in the past few days, she couldn't stomach the idea of the fawn dying a terrible death.

"No way, no how. I am not going to let whatever it is hurt you," she whispered. Searching around her, she found a large branch that, for one reason or another, wasn't covered with snow. She moved slowly, carefully, and picked it up then hefted it, judging its weight.

Hoping that the fawn could sense she was on her side, she lifted the branch over her head and circled the car. The Thing in the underbrush moved again and growled. Shay sucked in her gasp, rethought her idea, then forged ahead.

It's probably a rabbit. Yeah, like rabbits growl all the time.

Making a semicircle through the snow, she worked her way toward the brush, putting herself behind the predator. Once in position behind a large tree, she waited for it to move closer to the fawn.

If she hadn't thought it impossible, she would've guessed that the fawn was fascinated and knew what she had planned. The branch was heavy and its bark bit into her skin, but she held it firmly over her head, ready to react.

Everything happened at once. She saw the brush shaking as the animal broke through its branches and dashed toward the fawn. The fawn jumped into the air then spun around to bolt into the forest. As a large wolf rushed out of the forest, she brought down the branch as fast and as hard as she could. Her vision blurred in the same moment that she hit the animal. Shockwaves shuddered through her arms and she dropped the branch.

Shit.

Unable to control her body, she fell forward, darkness overcoming her.

Chapter Two

Rosh groaned and pushed over to face upward. He blinked at the sunlight as the ache in the back of his head seared a path along both sides of it. The snow against his back and rump didn't bother him. He'd always enjoyed the cold weather with or without clothing. But after chasing Kira for a mile in a game of hide-and-seek, the chill felt good.

Groaning again, he ran his palm over his hair and down to the curve of his neck, expecting to find the warm stickiness of blood, and yet found nothing. No doubt a knot would form soon enough even if the blow hadn't broken his skin.

What the crap hit me?

He let out a curse that was meant for both himself and the unseen assailant. He'd gotten so involved with playing with Kira that he hadn't paid attention to his surroundings. That was a bad mistake to make in either The Outside or in The Hidden.

Kira.

He sat up, ignoring the slashes of agony, and searched the area. Had the attacker taken the young one? If so, he'd spend his last breath finding her. He sniffed, trying to locate either Kira's human or fawn scent, but couldn't. He hoped she'd run off in time—especially before he'd shifted back to his human and *very* naked form—and was already well on her way back home.

Although shape-shifters were used to seeing everyone nude, young and old, he couldn't shake the uneasiness of being around a preteen girl while in his butt-naked human body and out like a light. He'd shifted into his wolf form behind a bush when Kira had begged him to play. She'd laughed at his shyness—after all, she'd grown up in The Hidden, and she was used to seeing everyone bare assed—but his conservative upbringing in Toledo, Ohio, was too difficult to shake.

Once again, he glanced around and saw no sign of her. She had to have gotten away.

A small form lay close by, the dark hair hiding the assailant's face. Her red jacket made a splash of color in the pristine snow. She was a lump on the ground, but there was no ignoring the body.

Her rounded bottom caught his attention. Her rump was the perfect size for a man to grab hold of as he plunged his cock deep inside her ass. The hair that hid her face was long and lustrous, urging him to run the silky strands between his fingers. Her legs were shapely even under the denim, and he wondered what treat was disguised by the bulky jacket she wore.

A woman had gotten the best of him? Even worse, a human woman? Humiliation mixed with the pounding of his headache. If the others got wind of the attack, he'd end up a laughingstock. He hoped Kira wouldn't say anything.

The woman moaned and moved a bit then stopped. He crawled over to her and leaned closer to take a big whiff. He'd expected her to smell like most women, but her aroma held an extra spice that entranced him. He drew in a longer breath, wanting more of her fragrance.

Damn, but she smells good. Like wildflowers on a sunny spring morning. Like the honey from a beehive with a taste of jalapeño pepper thrown in for an added pop of flavor.

She was spicy, sweet, with a good dose of female pheromones thrown in. He couldn't help himself. He skimmed his hand along the curve of her luscious butt cheek, paused, then squeezed it. She was firm yet pliable, exactly how he liked his women.

She moaned again, and he could easily imagine her moans of desire as he spanked her butt and slid his cock between the crease of her bottom and into the dark recess of her anus. He pulled his hand away reluctantly then took her by the shoulder and rolled her onto her back.

She's stunning.

He swept away the hair that covered one cheek and studied her oval face. She wouldn't win any beauty pageants by society's standards, but that was what made her so attractive to him. Instead of the flawless symmetry that movie stars and models strove to attain, her features spoke of intelligence and a maturity well past her years. Her body was fuller, riper than the skinny women most men found alluring. She had real breasts that were larger than his wide hands and pushed at the zipper of her coat. Her rounded stomach didn't flatten out even while she was on her back. She was all woman.

Damn. She's hurt. I'm gawking at her, and she's lying here hurt.

Guilt flashed through him, but he stubbornly pushed it away. It wasn't as though he was groping her without her knowledge like some kind of pervert.

Although I kind of did.

He thrust the thought away. He hadn't asked her to butt in. It was her own fault that she'd gotten hurt.

Dried blood formed around the injury to her forehead, but a fresh ribbon of blood oozed from it. She must've reopened a previous wound when she fell. He touched the gash to determine how deep it was and was relieved to find that it wasn't too bad. He unzipped her coat, telling himself that he needed to check her for any other signs of injury.

The jacket fell away from her generous breasts, and he had to struggle to take in air. The low-cut blouse she wore had shifted with her movements. One breast was fully exposed with her nipple peeking out from above the neckline of her shirt. Her brown areola was larger than most women's, and her nipple—due no doubt to the chill in the air—was pebbled. Saliva filled his mouth as he could almost feel the textured bud against his tongue as he licked the top of it and held it between his teeth.

Like the ultimate battle between good and evil, he struggled with his conscience. Was it his fault that her breast was exposed? Of course not. But he should cover her up. And he should do it fast, before his rising cock got the better of him and decided the outcome of the war.

Gritting his teeth, he pulled her jacket closed again. She wouldn't die from her wound, but unless he got her to shelter soon, she could wind up freezing to death before help came along.

He glanced at the car a few yards away. From the way the hood was bent toward the windshield, the vehicle had struck the large tree going at a good clip. She'd probably hit her head on the steering wheel then stumbled out of the car. Why she'd gone from stranded motorist to hunter he didn't know. But did it matter? He should be thinking of himself and not the woman who'd tried to take off half his head.

He snarled and pushed himself to his feet. If he had any sense at all, he'd haul her back to her car and leave her for someone else to find. Doing anything else would only make more trouble than he cared to handle.

He wasn't a do-gooder by any means. As a former assistant prosecuting attorney by profession, he'd had his fill of sad cases. All too often he'd gotten called into his boss's office and had been reamed out for letting his feelings get in the way of doing his best to win a case. But he couldn't help it. If he thought the defendant had gotten crappy breaks in life, he always tried to take it a little easier. Why kick a person when they were down? More than once he'd wondered if he'd ended up on the wrong side of the courtroom.

But that was before he'd found The Hidden. He'd heard about the mystical sanctuary for supernaturals, and, although he wasn't even sure it existed, he'd come into the mountains every year to search for it.

From what he'd heard from stories told throughout the werewolf community on The Outside, supernaturals found The Hidden through one of two ways. Either they knew someone who could show them the way, or they were able to sense the entrance whenever they came upon it. Rumored to be deep within the mountains, The Hidden's magical essence could be felt in the forest surrounding it.

During the second year, he'd run into Renkon, his cousin who had left home years earlier. He'd stumbled onto his cousin as he ran through the woods in his wolf form. The two had wrestled as they'd done as boys, rejoicing in seeing each other after so many years apart.

Once Rosh told him that he was seeking The Hidden, Renkon was more than delighted to show him the way. Renkon had found The Hidden on his own and had never returned to The Outside.

Renkon's description of the paradise-like place entranced Rosh and he'd followed Renkon into The Hidden. Aside from brief excursions like today, Rosh rarely went far from his new home.

He looked at the car then back to her. No way could he leave an injured woman alone. Who knew who or what might come across her? But what could he do? Take her down the mountain and get her help? Yet doing so would cause unwanted speculation as to how he'd found her. Plus, he didn't want her telling any stories about seeing a large wolf attacking an adorable deer. Stories of Red Riding Hood and Bambi would fill the media airwaves followed by a photo of her naked rescuer.

He only had one choice. He had to take her with him. The others wouldn't like it. As far as he knew, the only humans who were allowed into The Hidden were those who were going to mate a supernatural.

Grumbling, he took her by the arms and pulled her up. Her head lolled to the side in a sickening way that only reinforced his decision. Ducking down, he grabbed her ample bottom and pushed her limp body onto his shoulders. He settled her against him, made certain that his hold on her was secure, then strode into the woods.

* * * *

Shay had suffered through her share of headaches, but the one pounding inside her head was the worst she'd ever had. Add that to the constant bouncing of her body against a hard surface and she was sure she'd either pass out again or upchuck.

She opened her eyes, struggling against the pain behind them, and saw the ground moving underneath her at an incredible rate. Whoever, *whatever* was holding her moved faster than humanly possible.

Fear gripped her even as the sight of a bare butt enticed her to blink and take a better look. The man's hind end was firm and strong. Muscles moved under the bronzed skin, and a patch of dark hair led her gaze to the crack between the cheeks.

She flattened her hands against his back and pushed her body away from his then lifted her head. Maybe she could get a good look at her…her what? Her rescuer? Or her abductor?

"Hey! Whoever you are, put me down!"

She started to pound against his back then stopped. What good would it do anyway? His back was as solid as a wall of granite and flexed with every step he took then tapered down to his delectable buttocks. If she got the chance, she'd love to pinch his butt then run her tongue over the smooth surface.

Shit. How can I think about sex when I'm being hauled around like a side of beef? A nauseous side of beef that might lose it at any moment?

She dug her nails into his skin. If she couldn't impede his progress by demanding he put her down, then the least she could do was inflict a little pain. Yet he didn't seem to notice even when she managed to lay down long scratches.

Her hair flopped in front of her face as she tried to regulate her breathing. If she didn't get him to stop soon, she wasn't sure what would happen except that it wouldn't be pleasant for either one of them.

"If you don't put me down real fast, you're going to be sorry."

She got a response from him, but it wasn't the one she'd wanted. Who chuckles when they're threatened?

Struggling against him, she wiggled as much as she could, but that only resulted in his tightening his hold on her. At last, she couldn't hold it back any longer.

"I–I'm going to—"

She tried to choke her vomit back but couldn't. Giving up, she opened her mouth and spewed her last meal down his back and over his awesome butt.

"Shit!"

He skidded to a stop, jostling her even more. Another wave of sickness swept over her as he bent over and dumped her to the ground. She hurled again, this time managing to turn her head away from him.

Dry heaving now, she jolted when he took her hair and held it back. He knelt beside her, dipped his hand into the clean snow, and cupped his hand. Holding out the fresh snow, he offered it to her.

She hadn't dared to look up and, instead, studied the sparkling fluff in the palm of his hand. Embarrassment swamped her, making her forget that she'd warned him.

Drinking like a forest creature from a stream, she flicked out her tongue, sweeping up a bit of the snow. It felt cool inside her mouth and washed away the grime.

"Use a little to wash around your mouth. Especially your chin."

She still couldn't look him in the eye, but oh, how she loved his voice. Like a medicine all its own, his rich, deep timbre flowed over her, warming her body like an electric blanket on a winter morning. Taking a dab of the snow, she did as he suggested.

"Are you better?"

Why was he being so nice to her? Was that how kidnappers were supposed to treat their victims? Why haul her ass off only to help her when she got sick?

"I'm sorry."

Aw, crap. Now he's apologizing? What's with this guy? Yet she couldn't help but give him a piece of her mind.

"You should be. What the fuck do you think you're doing? Are you kidnapping me?" She lifted her head, letting her anger and embarrassment form her defiance. Yet when she looked into his dark eyes, she lost every thought except one.

He's amazing.

His eyes were only the start of him. Straight black hair drifted forward to caress his high cheekbones. His nose, slightly crooked, led to a mouth that was surrounded by stubble. His jawline was the kind only leading men had while his chin jutted out, proudly pronouncing him a dominant, take-charge kind of guy.

She dropped her gaze down his wide, harder-than-a-diamond chest to his ripped stomach. If she dared to touch him, she knew she could ram her fist into his stomach and he probably wouldn't even notice. No wonder he'd chuckled at her feeble attempts to get free. He made every other man look like a ninety-pound weakling.

Swallowing, she did the only thing she could do. To not do it would be an insult to womankind everywhere. She let her gaze slide even lower.

Oh. My. God. Is he really that big? Or am I hallucinating?

"Consider the apology rescinded. I thought I was helping you."

"Helping me? By kidnapping me?"

He took a deep breath, expanding his already-huge chest. What would it be like to have that chest hovering over her?

"No, I'm not. But never mind about that. Do you feel better?"

She blinked and tried to make sense of his words. How could anyone expect her to think with that battering ram pointing at her? "What?"

"I asked you if you're feeling better."

She brought her attention back to his incredible face. "Oh. Yeah. I guess so."

"Good. Then maybe you can tell me what the fuck you were thinking?"

"Huh?"

He scooped up a large amount of snow, stood, and started washing the results of her upset stomach off his back and rump. Even in his current soiled condition, she couldn't help but run her tongue over her upper lip. Once he cleaned himself up, would she dare to drag her tongue along the rippling muscle? Maybe around to the front of him and over his huge cock?

"Uh, I'm sorry."

He glared at her.

"You know. For upchucking on you. Not for anything else."

"Yeah, that made my day. But pay attention. I want to know what you were thinking when you hit me."

"I hit you?" She frowned, trying to remember. She'd run off the road to swerve away from something in the road, but there was no way this hunk of a male specimen was that scrawny thing.

"Yeah, you did."

She shook her head and came to her feet, albeit a bit wobbly. He grasped her by the arm and kept her steady. Suddenly she wished she was naked, too, so she could feel the touch of his hand on her arm.

"No, I didn't. I saw an animal or whatever in the road, and I stupidly tried to miss it, which sent my car into the trees." She turned around, only now taking the time to see where they were.

The forest lay behind them as they stood in a tiny clearing. She pivoted around and stared at the open expanse before her. Taking a step forward, she was grateful that he still held on to her.

They stood at the precipice of a cliff overlooking a roaring waterfall. A river rushed below them, the white caps of the waves testifying to the speed and power of the current. On the far side of the divide, the forest spread out and led up the mountainside.

"Wow."

"What did you see in the road?"

The serious tone of his voice caught her, sinking fear into her heart. His hold tightened on her, causing her to whine against her will.

"I don't know. I can't really remember what it looked like. Hell, I'm not even sure I got a good look at it. It had red eyes, I remember that, and it was thin. Really thin."

"And then you crashed into the tree."

She nodded, confirming his words that weren't a question. Carefully, she pulled her arm away. "Yeah. I think I conked out for a bit. Then I got out of my car, and that's when I saw this enormous wolf about to attack a poor little fawn."

He let out a long breath. "And you thought you could take down a wolf?"

His frustration was evident in his snarl. "Okay, I admit it wasn't my best idea. But I wasn't thinking very clearly right then, you know?"

"Yeah, I know."

She had to stop thinking with her libido. Granted, he was hot as hell, but he was still a stranger who had slung her over his shoulder and taken off with her. A *naked* stranger. She stepped away, putting a few feet between them.

"Where do you think you're going?"

What do the experts say about handling kidnappers? Keep them calm?

"Look, I appreciate you, uh, carrying me, but I'm going back to my car. I think I'll have a better chance of someone finding me there."

"Not now you won't." He glanced toward the setting sun that was coloring the sky with purples and blues.

If they'd met under different circumstances, the sunset might've seemed romantic. As it was, she knew he was right. Trying to go back to her car through God knew how big a forest was a bad idea. But what choice did she have?

"You'll have to come with me."

"I don't think so." Going with a stranger was bad enough, but a naked stranger who hung out—literally—in the woods? Not a chance. "Why don't you have any clothes, anyway? Is this Montana's answer to the annual polar bear swim?"

"The what?"

"You know. That ritual where normally sane people go swimming in the middle of winter in ice-cold water."

"So you think I'm insane? But no, that's got nothing to do with this. You'll find out soon enough."

Is that a threat or a promise? I think now's the time to get the hell out of here.

She turned and ran even though she knew she'd never outrun him. He caught her before she'd gotten ten feet.

"Calm down. I'm doing this to save your hide." He grabbed her jacket and tugged her out of it.

Panic took over, but she was no match for his strength. She struggled, fear clogging her throat so she couldn't scream. Tossing her jacket aside, he ripped her blouse from her in one quick move.

Shay struck out as he took her arm and tugged her closer to the edge. She broke free, but he snatched her up by the waist and put her ass flat on the ground. Kicking him was like swatting a dinosaur with a stick. He got her boots and socks off without much trouble then took hold of the top of her jeans and yanked them down her legs. She lay shivering in the snow as he threw them over the side of the cliff. He bent over her, and she struck out, hitting him in the face.

He jerked his head away then confronted her again, the snarl bigger than before. Growling, he reached out and tore her panties off. "I told you to calm down. Don't you ever listen?"

His voice sounded calm and determined, but she saw a flash of heat in his eyes. Was it anger or lust? Was he going to rape her? Then what? Leave her to freeze during the night?

"Hang on to me. I don't want you to get hurt." He tugged her to her feet then picked her up and carried her even closer to the drop over the waterfall.

"Please. Don't."

His strong arms pressed against her breasts as he held her in front of him. She continued to struggle against him. She doubted she'd get free, but she was damned sure going to go down fighting.

"Relax. You've got this all wrong." He tightened his arms around her, keeping her back to his chest. "Close your eyes. It's not as scary that way."

"What are you talking about?"

If he answered her, she never heard it over the scream ripping out of her throat. Holding her tightly, he jumped off the cliff, taking her with him.

Chapter Three

"You had no right to bring her here."

Charlton, the oldest of The Hidden's council members and considered one of the wisest men in the community, didn't motion for Rosh to take a seat on the ground before them. His white beard touched his chest and his mustache covered his mouth. Wise blue eyes shone with intelligence, and he held on to a cane everyone knew he didn't really need for support.

Charlton had long ago given up his life as the mayor of a small town in California on The Outside to live in The Hidden. His leadership abilities had quickly earned him a place on the ruling council. In The Hidden, he no longer had to hide that fact that he was a werewolf.

"I didn't have a choice." Rosh hadn't had time to figure out what he was going to say. He'd arrived less than an hour before with the unconscious woman. Then as soon as the women saw her condition they'd whisked her into Rosh's hut and had called their best healer, Penn, to care for her. Although most supernaturals could heal themselves, they found it necessary at times to enlist her help. Penn's skills had healed the gash on Shay's head then she'd given her a sleeping potion so she would rest peacefully for a day or two.

After checking to make sure Kira was back with her mother, he'd answered the summons of The Council. Now he wished he'd come up with an excuse and given himself time to prepare for their interrogation.

"There's always a choice." Xnax, one of the native residents of The Hidden and one of the oldest shape-shifters who could change into any animal he wished, played with the fire in front of him. His belly protruded outward from his skinny body, giving him the appearance of being pregnant. He passed his gnarled hand with five-inch nails that were as black as his eyes over the flames. Snatching at the air, he caught a ball of fire, bounced it in his hand, then tossed it back into the fire.

"Xnax is right. You should've left her where she was." Tina, the youngest and only female member of The Council, met his gaze. Her silver eyes held the hint of playfulness that all fairies possessed.

Two other members of The Council, a werewolf and a werecat, nodded in agreement.

"No, I couldn't. The road was impassable by then, and no one would have found her before the cold took her limbs and, possibly, her life." He slid his gaze over the row of leaders. "Leaving her alone would have left her defenseless against Burac."

They remained silent, taking in his words. He was right, and they knew it. The rule had always been to never bring a human into The Hidden without the sole purpose of mating with him or her. Once the human agreed to mate, he or she could choose to remain human or to change.

Those humans foolish enough to get stranded in the woods on The Outside and who were not intended as mates had always been left to their fate. But since Burac, leader of The Cursed, had started going to The Outside, things had changed. They couldn't and wouldn't allow him to take a human into his pack. To keep him from doing so, they'd help the person find their way out of the forest without giving them any clue about The Hidden's existence.

"What's done is done." Charlton added more wrinkles to his face with his scowl. "The question is what to do with her now."

"We could keep her locked in the basement of one of the cabins. Then, when The Time of Leaving comes again, Rosh can blindfold her and take her down the mountain. She wouldn't be allowed to see our people or our home."

"It will be a few more weeks before anyone can drive safely on the road. Keeping her locked up will be difficult. She might not be able to see anything, but she would hear us."

"What does it matter if she sees or hears us? No one on The Outside will believe her."

"Then we're back where we began." Tina tossed her blue hair behind her shoulders.

He had to make them let her stay. If he had to, he'd risk his reputation for her. He didn't understand why, but he sensed she was special. The way she'd glared at him, the way she'd spoken to him had excited him. But the way she'd clung to him, terrified yet thrilled, as he'd taken her over the waterfall had intrigued him. He wanted to find out more about her.

"I think I may want her as my mate."

The words were out of his mouth and gone before he'd given them a thought. What was he saying? He didn't know the woman, and yet he was pledging his life to her?

"You *think* you may want her?" Xnax laughed. "Our people don't *think* they want someone. They know it when they meet."

"Then I know it." *Hell and damnation, why can't I keep my trap shut?*

Charlton's knowing gaze made him look away. "Fine. We'll give you a week. If you're certain by then and she has found at least one other to mate with her, then we'll meet again and discuss the situation further."

"Renkon wants her, too." What the hell was wrong with him? Not only had he committed himself, he'd tied his cousin to her. Of course, she was the one who would decide to mate them or not. If they weren't right for each other, she'd refuse them and everything would return to normal again. Hopefully, she'd be allowed to choose different mates.

"Very well then. But you're responsible for her. Make sure she doesn't stir up any trouble." Tina's wings popped out from her back, a sign that she was excited. "If you want her to stir up anything else, then go right ahead."

* * * *

Shay fell, her arms flailing around her as she tried to grab on to air. The man who'd thrown his body into space with his arms wrapped around her fell in front of her. His back was to the water, and he plastered on an insane smile. His smile turned into laughter as he flung out his arms and spread his legs wide.

She screamed and reached for him, but he was going too fast for her to catch up. The water approached them faster by the second. Her mind refused to believe what he'd done even as her heart clenched with terror. They'd hit the water moving too fast for any human to survive the impact.

She closed her eyes, remembering what he'd said, then opened them again, too frightened not to look. But he was gone. In his place was a huge black wolf. The wolf, his back to the water as the man's had been, opened its mouth to expose treacherous fangs. Its tongue lolled out as its mouth spread into a smile that reminded her of the man's.

Shay sat up, a scream caught in her throat, her arms outstretched as they'd been in the nightmare. But she wasn't anywhere near the water. With her heart thundering in her ears, she glanced around her then pulled the brightly colored blanket up to her neck. She peeked underneath it and found that she wore a dress of a soft material that she didn't recognize. After skimming her hand over her body, she didn't think she was injured. Lifting her fingers to her forehead, she was amazed to find the gash in her head gone.

Where am I?

Bright light spilling in from a hole in the roof formed a circle on the dirt floor next to the oversized bed that was made of more blankets piled on top of one another. The material reminded her of silk, but the vibrant hues looked as though they were a natural part of the fabric and not a result of any dye. Taking up a large portion of the one-room interior of the hut, the bed was large enough to accommodate several people.

The walls of the hut were made of dried clay or mud while she guessed that the roof was made of branches and straw. Smooth bowls made of wood were lined against the far wall, and candles that were more resplendent than any she'd seen in high-end boutiques were stacked on top of each other next to the bowls. A flap extending across a wide portion of one wall served as a door.

"Why did you bring her here?"

"I've already told you why. I didn't have a choice. What should I have done? Left her alone? You know what could've happened."

She recognized the man's voice as the one who'd taken her. Yet even now she couldn't get past the impression that he'd done so to help her and not to cause her any harm. Other than risking her neck by diving off a cliff and into a waterfall.

"I understand, Rosh, but I'm not sure everyone else will. Impromptu visitors aren't exactly commonplace, you know."

"Let me handle it. I've already spoken with The Council."

"Well, at least if you had to drag a woman home, you picked a good one. I think I almost came when we were getting the dress on her. She's got curves that just won't stop."

Warmth that had nothing to do with shyness took over. But who was the other man? And where had Rosh taken her?

"Keep your hands off her until we know what we're going to do."

The other man chuckled. "I will if you will. But I wouldn't take any bets on it."

"One other thing. I'm responsible for her."

"Are you saying you told them—"

"Yeah. I didn't have any other choice. And you, too."

"Me? Why'd you do that, Rosh?"

"I couldn't leave you out of it. They know we plan to do it

together."

"But that's not our decision alone."

"Which might be our way out of this situation."

"I see what you mean. But thanks anyway for playing roulette with my life."

"No problem, Renkon. That's what cousins are for."

She heard their footsteps as they walked away. It had been almost dark when they'd made the leap into the water, but the sun was shining and she could feel the warmth in the air. In fact, if she didn't know better, she'd swear it was springtime outside.

Throwing the cover off, she crawled over to the door flap and peeked outside. Yet she wasn't sure she wasn't still dreaming. Snow no longer covered the ground. Instead, green grass and an abundance of flowers of various types and colors surrounded what looked like a campground. Other huts, some larger, some smaller, dotted the perimeter, along with teepees. Canvas tents straight out of the local sporting-goods store were scattered between the huts. Even more astonishing, a few cabins with porches boasting several rocking chairs sat farther back, closer to where the valley led into the mountainside.

Shay dropped the flap and tried to make sense of it all. Where had he taken her? Even the lower levels of Montana didn't look like this in the winter. Had he taken her over state lines? Had she really been abducted and transported to another, albeit warmer, place?

And what kind of community lived in everything from cabins to mud huts? She peeked out again. What kind of place had homes like these but no people? She scanned the area, checking for any signs of life. The place looked lived in yet deserted.

Stop wasting time.

She grabbed a pair of moccasin-style shoes next to the opening and slipped them on her feet. They fit perfectly, reminding her of a pair she'd had as a child. Gathering her resolve, she pulled the flap back and got ready to run.

She didn't even make it out of the tent before a grand buck

blocked her way. It shook its head, waving the points of its antlers in front of her. She yelped and fell backward then crab crawled as quickly as she could back inside. After taking a moment to regain her breath, she tugged back the flap again, determined to face what had to be another hallucination. The buck was still there, pawing at the ground and snorting.

She'd seen enough photographs of ill-fated campers who'd tried to take on a buck to know she couldn't get past it. But she wasn't about to give up. Come hell or high water, or even a big buck standing outside the hut, she was getting out.

The sun on the tip of her nose gave her an idea. She gazed up at the hole in the roof then stood and studied its width. Although she'd always been considered plump, her weight had never bothered her. Instead, she'd focused on enjoying life and not worrying about what others thought. But at that exact moment, she suddenly wished she'd joined a weight-loss program.

If she could squeeze through the opening, she could jump out, putting the hut between her and the buck. It wouldn't be much of a head start, but she hoped it would be enough. If she had to, she'd hightail it to one of the cabins and pound on the door until someone let her in. They might have a phone she could use to call for help.

But what if she got stuck in the opening? She pushed the idea away. Having chosen to be an optimist most of her life, she wasn't about to let doubt sideline her now. The only problem was how she could heft her body high enough to pull herself through the hole.

Could she stack the bowls? Would they hold her weight? The only way to find out was to try. She hurriedly took one bowl after another, turned them upside down, and stacked them as high and as wide as she could. The resulting structure didn't look very stable, but it would have to do.

Carefully, she put her foot on the first bowl, took a breath, and hopped, reaching for the rim of the hole as she balanced on top of her shaky sculpture. She let out a small cry of victory and pulled her upper torso through the hole.

She took a quick look, saw that the buck had his head down in front of the flap, and knew she'd caught a lucky break. Flattening her hands on the top, she heaved the rest of her body through the hole until she could sit with her legs hanging inside. She grinned and started to swing her right leg out of the opening.

"Ayyy!"

* * * *

Rosh yanked on the woman's leg and pulled her back through the opening. As before, she wasn't going to make things easy on him as she kicked and struck out. Avoiding a punch that almost clocked him in the jaw, he dropped her, letting her land on her butt. How many times would he have to toss her on her ass before she'd stop fighting him?

He fell on top of her before she could scramble away and pushed her to her back. Holding her arms around her head by her wrists, he put his face close to hers. She froze, her big brown eyes widening as he settled his body over hers without resting his entire weight on top of her.

Her tantalizing scent drifted into his nostrils, and he dragged in a deep breath, closing his eyes for one moment to savor the aroma. He opened his eyes again and let his gaze fall to her chest, hidden under the modest dress she wore, as it rose and fell, making him choose between watching the swell of her breasts and studying the fullness of her lips. Her lush body molded against his, and he knew in that instant that he never wanted to let her go.

Her mouth parted as she peeked the tip of her tongue out. Was she trying to drive him insane? His cock was already straining against his jeans. If he dared kiss her, he wouldn't have a chance of restraining himself.

"Turn me loose."

If only she'd keep her mouth shut.

Yet another part of him, the side that enjoyed a spirited woman, rejoiced. She was irritating and stubborn, but she was fiery and every inch a woman. "Where do you think you're going to go?"

"Home."

"Trust me. You'd never make it." She had no clue where she was, but he wasn't ready to tell her. Not until she'd agreed to stop trying to run off. If she did, he wouldn't be able to protect her, but he doubted she'd understand that.

"You want me to trust you? Are you fucking kidding me?"

He'd never liked women who cussed, but she made it seem sexy. "Nope."

She narrowed her eyes, obviously trying to decide whether she should believe him. "What are you talking about? Why the hell did you bring me here? Where am I anyway?"

"Once you promise not to run away, I'll explain that to you later."

"Why not now?"

He smiled and then, unable to stand it any longer, he put his mouth close to her ear and whispered, "Do you always get whatever you want whenever you want it?"

He bit down on her earlobe just enough to sting but not enough to hurt. She gasped but didn't attempt to move away.

"Well, yeah. If I have any say about it. Doesn't everyone? Are you planning on chomping my earlobe off?"

She jerked her head to the side, pulling his teeth off her ear then cupping her hand over it. "Shit, man. A bit animalistic, don't you think?"

"So you're a princess, huh?"

He tilted his head, daring her to deny his accusation. She didn't. Instead, she dropped her gaze down the length of their bodies.

Was she trying to see his erection? He let a small smile escape. "Can't you feel that I want you?"

Her gaze whipped back to his, then pointedly glanced down then up again. "Trust me. *It's* no big deal."

He let his body push against hers a little harder then worked his leg between hers. "Is that so? If it's not, then why are you hot against my leg? Hell, I can feel your juices through my jeans."

Surprise then shyness flitted across her face until her brash nature came back in full force. "Don't flatter yourself."

"What's your name?"

"What?"

His abrupt change in the conversation had thrown her. "I asked you your name. After all we've been through, don't you think we should know each other's names?"

"Sure. I need to know who to tell the police to lock up."

He laughed then pushed his leg harder against her crotch. She inhaled again, and, for a moment, he thought she might wrap her legs around his waist. He was disappointed when she didn't. "I'm Rosh McClain. And you?"

She blinked then whispered the name he'd longed to hear since finding her unconscious by his side. "Shay. Shay Mathews. Now get off me."

"Shay. I like it. It fits you."

"I'm so glad you approve."

Her sarcasm was as enchanting as her wit. "You've slept for two days, but I see it hasn't improved your disposition."

"Two days? No. That can't be." She struggled against him then gave up.

"You took a good knock on the head. But don't worry. You've already healed." He widened his smile then lowered to kiss the sweet swell of her breast. "Not that your wound stopped you for long."

Was it his imagination, or was she taking deeper breaths? He slid his tongue from one breast to the other. His body hummed with need as he searched her eyes and found the answer he'd hoped for. She wanted him as much as he wanted her.

"Look, Mr. McClain—"

"Shh. And the name's Rosh."

"Rosh, you've got to take me back to my car."

"I'll think about it. If you're a good girl."

He could see that she recognized a line when she heard one.

He turned her wrists loose and caressed her cheek before taking her by the chin. "Show me how good you can be, Shay."

He kissed her then, giving into the sexual tug that had fired to life when he'd plopped her on the ground and pulled off her clothes. He'd hated that she'd reacted as though he was going to rape her, but he hadn't had the time to explain. The only way into The Hidden was through the water and only during specific time periods, including when they'd arrived at the top of the waterfall. If she'd jumped with her clothes on, the weight of the water soaking into her clothes would've dragged her to the bottom.

But that no longer mattered. He'd explain in time. All that mattered now was the softness of her lips. Her mouth opened to his like a rose opening to a new day, and he slipped his hand under the hem of her dress. His hand skimmed over her smooth skin, moving upward to take her breast even as he relished the sensation of her body pressed close to his.

He gently slipped his tongue into her mouth and waited for her reaction, letting her take the lead since he'd had to force her to go with him into The Hidden. He'd done it for her, but he doubted she'd see it that way. At least, not at first.

To his joy, she answered his kiss with a touch of her tongue to his, then a hard suck as she dragged his inside her mouth. Rosh groaned, forcing back his inner wolf, who howled to be set free and claim her. If he hadn't already realized how much he wanted her, his other half told him so now. He rolled to his side, holding her firmly as he tracked his fingers into her long, silky mane. It was as soft as he'd dreamed it would be for the past two nights.

The dreams had tormented him, keeping him and his cousin, Renkon, away from their small home to sleep on the ground beside the hut. When she'd moaned in her fitful sleep, he and Renkon had taken turns, argued for turns, in fact, to soothe her fevered brow with a cool cloth. The women, among them Kira's mother, Myla, had bathed her, but he wouldn't let them take over her care. Although it wasn't a man's place to tend to a woman, he and Renkon had stood against tradition.

He stroked her hair, breaking the kiss so he could search her face. Her eyes were lidded, the muscles of her face relaxed as she gave herself over to him. How had he not recognized her from the very start? To think that he might've never met her had he not played with Kira churned in his gut. But it was the thought of what had driven her from the road that made his blood run cold.

He forced the worry away for later. For now, he would relish his time with her.

"Rosh?"

"Yes, Shay?"

She started to speak her mind then stopped. "Nothing."

"No. This is definitely something." He brought his mouth to hers, plundering her mouth with a barely restrained fervor. Lying with her, without even taking her yet, had changed sex for him forever. He had a feeling that she'd changed him forever.

She pushed against his chest and made him lean away from her. "I don't know you."

"You will. If I have anything to say about it, you will." He'd meant what he'd said, but the cautious side of him shouted for him to stop promising her more than that very moment together. But he'd think about that tomorrow.

He tugged the top of her dress lower, caught a nipple between his teeth, and reenacted part of his dream. She groaned and bowed her back, thrusting her breasts toward him. The simple act almost made him come, but when she lifted her leg, moving her dress higher on her thigh then placing her leg on top of his, he was sure he wouldn't last much longer. He flicked his tongue between her breasts, tugging at first one then the other nipple.

He pulled the hem higher and cupped her bare mons. As most of the women in The Hidden did, she wore no underwear. If he could stand it, he would give her pleasure first. If he didn't, he was afraid that once he sank his cock deep inside her pussy, he'd lose all control and fuck her like a wild animal.

He slipped two fingers between her folds and found her pussy, hot and wet, ready for him. His palm lay against the soft curls, and he swore before long he'd bury his nose between her legs and drink in her scent as well as her flavor.

A vision of Renkon sucking on her breasts as he feasted on her pussy shuddered through him, but for now, he would take her without his cousin. Those in The Hidden coupled with more than one, usually three men to one woman, and, although he'd have no problem sharing her with his cousin, he wasn't as sure about another man. Could he stand someone other than Renkon tugging on her nipple? Would he enjoy seeing another man rut her from behind? Or would the jealous twinge inside him grow stronger? But he'd worry about that tomorrow, too.

Her clit pulsed against his fingers as he began to massage the sensitive area. She lay back and spread her legs wider, and he followed her without turning her pussy loose. Rubbing her clit in alternating hard then soft circles, he watched as she tugged the top of her dress under her breasts. The material supported her full tits, making them seem even larger and plumper.

"Finger-fuck me." She clutched her breasts, mimicking his circular motions with her thumbs on her nipples.

He shoved a finger into her pussy, and her mouth fell open in a silent cry. She was so damn beautiful, radiant in the throes of sex. Her pussy walls clamped around his finger, giving him a preview of how fucking wonderful she'd feel once he replaced his finger with his cock.

"Harder. More."

He added another finger and rammed them inside as hard as he could. His palm slapped against the skin between her cunt and her butt hole. She lifted her head then laid it back and threw it side to side as her body shuddered under his touch. Warmth flooded over his hand as she bucked, trying to get away as her climax tore through her.

He moved between her legs, shoving his jeans down to his ankles. Lifting her legs so she could wrap them around his waist, he positioned his cock to tease the opening of her pussy. Unable to hold back a moment more, he plunged into her, sinking his cock into her sweet, hot core. He grabbed her ass cheeks, sinking his fingers into her skin. She cried out, but he could no more stop fucking her than he could've stopped the moon from rising.

He sank into her, harder, faster, needing her more than ever. Her soft *uhs* turned him on even more, and, impossibly, he felt his shaft grow bigger. She was a mesmerizing temptress, and he was her willing servant.

If he could've stopped, could've found a way to slow down, he would have. But as it was, he needed her too much.

She lifted onto her elbows and thrust her pelvis forward, giving him everything he gave her and more. Growling, he fell onto his back, taking her with him. Unlike most of his kind, he didn't think having the woman on top meant he wasn't the dominant one. It simply meant he could sink his cock even deeper inside her.

She took the shirt he had worn just for her and, to his surprise and delight, tore it open. She took hold of his pecs as he did her breasts. Her long hair drifted over her breasts that were still held by her dress, giving him an erotic show.

He pounded into her, getting her to make the mewling sounds again. She rode him, bucking on top of him like a sexy rider determined not to get bucked off. Her ass met his flesh to make a satisfying sucking noise.

The orgasm that he'd managed to hold back would no longer be denied. His balls drew up and his seed rolled toward the finish. He held on to her tighter and rammed against her as hard as he could, his panting sounds mixing with hers. With a growl that turned into a groan, he let loose, shooting his cum into her pussy. His body shuddered, jerking out the remainder of his cum.

She stayed on top of him, her hair draped over her chest, her mouth parted and her eyes softened with desire. Slowly, his cock softened, and she slumped forward to put her head against his chest. Turning on his side again, he rested her on her back and smiled as she cuddled against him.

She traced patterns on his chest as he turned to place a kiss on her forehead. "You know this doesn't change anything."

He pulled back to look at her. "What are you talking about?"

"I'm still getting out of here. With or without your help."

Rosh sat up, pushing her to the side then tugging his jeans up and his shirt together. "Like hell you are. You're staying put until I say you can leave."

She sat up and pulled her dress to cover her body. Her eyes flashed with anger as she poked a finger against his chest.

"Look, Tarzan. Nobody tells me what to do. I've already overlooked your earlier caveman routine, tossing me over your shoulder and all, but you've pushed my patience as far as it's going to go."

Even now she made his cock twitch with need. But he had to make sure she stayed where she was. "You will or else."

He was stunned when she laughed at him. "Or else what?"

Reaching behind him, he stuck his hand into a large basket that contained several items and drew out a long piece of rope. "Or else I'll have to tie you up."

Her mouth dropped open. "You're not serious."

"Believe me, I am." He hated having to force her, but she didn't realize the danger she'd face if she left without him. And he couldn't take her back yet. The Time of Leaving hadn't come yet. "I don't want to, but I will for your own good."

"What the hell does that mean?"

She was a spitfire, and he loved it. But he had to keep her safe. He had to explain things to her. "I'm not trying to order you around—"

Her arched eyebrow challenged his statement.

"Okay, so maybe I am, but I'm not doing it for my benefit. I don't want to see you hurt. Haven't I proven that already by bringing you here?"

"Oh, sure. Dragging me into the wilderness hundreds of miles away says you care better than a Hallmark card."

"You're not hundreds of miles away. And if I hadn't taken you with me, you'd have been lucky to get back to town with all your toes and fingers intact." The conversation was getting out of control, but he was damned if he could figure out how to get it back on track.

"Are you saying this is Montana? It was snowing at the bottom of the mountain as well as where I ditched my car."

She thought he'd taken her out of the state. How else could she explain the difference in the weather? They'd left a snowbound area and wound up in a spring-like setting complete with greenery and warm weather.

"You're going to find this hard to believe, but keep an open mind."

"Rosh! Get out here."

He turned toward the sound of Renkon's shout. His cousin had always had lousy timing. He hated to leave things unresolved, but he had no time to tell her about The Hidden. "What's it going to be, Shay? Are you staying on your own accord, or am I trussing you up?"

The desire she'd shown him earlier was gone, replaced by a cold fury. "Fine. For now, I'll do as you say."

"Good. I'll send one of the other women to tend to you." With that said, he stood and strode out of the tent.

* * * *

What the hell just happened?

Shay shivered, but it was a good feeling and not one coming from fear. She put her palm to her chest and felt her heart still pounding. As though she'd had no control, she'd opened her legs for the man who had taken her, and yet, she didn't feel anything but a strange sense of joy.

Had she lost her common sense when she'd banged her head in the accident? She didn't think so. Fact was, she didn't even like the idea of thinking that could be the reason she'd given in so fast.

She bit her lower lip. What she'd done with Rosh would never have happened before she'd met him. She wouldn't have lain with a man she'd met only hours—correction, two days—earlier. Especially a man who'd slung her over his back and abducted her. Granted, he may have saved her life, but the way he'd gone about it was out of line.

Then why did she get a thrill every time she thought about it? She'd always found macho men, men who took a woman when they wanted and how they wanted, sexy as hell. Providing it wasn't rape, of course. But what they'd done was nowhere near a rape. She'd been a very willing participant and, even now, she couldn't wait to do it again.

What was it about this guy that made her want to hold him, to cuddle against him, then ride him until she couldn't sit up a moment longer?

Wow. I've lost it big time.

She pressed her fingers to her thoroughly kissed lips and felt the warmth of her cream between her legs.

If this is losing it, I hope I never find it again. But what now? Is it a one-time thing? A wilderness fuck and run?

She jutted out her chin. If it was, then so be it. But her bravado never reached her heart.

Concentrate on getting your ass home.

She'd gotten so involved in her feelings that she hadn't noticed the conversation going on right outside the hut.

She pulled the tent flap back, too curious not to see who had called to him. The great buck was gone, but Rosh wasn't with only one person. He stood with two other men, both as tall and as powerful as he was.

One of them was similar to Rosh in appearance with the same black hair and stubble running over his upper lip and covering his jaw. His hair was a bit shorter, but his shoulders were as wide and solid as Rosh's. He was dressed in only jeans, leaving his magnificent upper torso bare and his feet without shoes. He spoke to Rosh, moving his hands to emphasize whatever he was saying.

Why does he look familiar? Have I met him before? She didn't think so, but she was certain this wasn't the first time she'd seen his face.

"You know we're supposed to get approval from The Council before bringing a woman here."

"Like I told you before. I didn't have any other choice, Renkon."

"Although I can't say that I'm too upset. She's different. I could see that even though she was asleep."

So he'd seen her asleep, too? She should've felt afraid, but she didn't. Instead, she found the idea of two gorgeous men watching over her hot as hell. Had the third man seen her, too?

He didn't look like Rosh. Although he had dark hair and eyes, his wavy hair was kept short. He, too, wore the rugged stubble along his face, but his skin was darker, making her think he was of Hispanic descent. Slightly shorter than Rosh and Renkon, he stood with his arms crossed over his shirtless chest and silently listened to the other two men speak. He, too, seemed familiar, like someone from a distant memory or a dream that she couldn't recall.

When at last he spoke, his voice held the hint of an accent. "I saw her, too."

Rosh turned on him, his voice growing louder, his tone one of command. "Let it go, Walker."

Walker smiled, but it held no warmth. "That's not our way, and you know it. You may have brought her here, but that doesn't mean I can't want her to choose me, too."

Her eyes grew wide. What did he mean by that? Had she unknowingly already chosen Rosh? If so, for what? Did she want to choose anyone? Why did she get the sinking feeling that some hillbilly was about to show up with a shotgun?

"Bullshit." Rosh took a step forward, his dare evident in his clenched fist.

"Calm down, man. He's right. Besides, she's the one who makes the final decision."

"Listen to your cousin. He's got it straight. Why don't we ask her right now?" Yet Walker didn't move.

"She doesn't know anything yet, and she can't make an informed decision until she does."

Walker's smile grew. "Then let's tell her."

"Not yet. She's been through enough for now."

She'd realized Rosh was holding back information. Crouching, she started to throw back the flap so she could storm out and demand answers. But Rosh's next move stopped her cold.

He snarled and shoved Walker's shoulder. Walker lurched toward him, but Renkon jumped in between them and held them apart. After a few moments of exchanging glares with Rosh, Walker turned on his heel and stalked away.

Rosh broke free of his cousin's hold and stalked off in the opposite direction. Renkon rested his fists on his waist and shook his head. "Damn it, Rosh. Think with the head on your shoulders."

She couldn't help it. She had to giggle at Renkon's remark. When she did, he swiveled in her direction. Startling blue eyes, so unlike Rosh's dark ones, hooked onto her. She fell backward and let the flap fall closed.

"Holy shit, Shay. What have you gotten yourself into now?"

Chapter Four

Shay had never given much credence to sayings, but she was betting on the old "the third time's the charm" phrase. If she didn't get away tonight, she'd take it as fate and stick it out until Rosh delivered on his promise to take her back to her car.

Peeking out the flap, she watched as more and more people arrived. Men, women, and children poured into the campground and greeted each other with friendly slaps on the backs, hugs, and kisses. They were from different ethnicities as well as shapes and sizes. The women all wore the same type of dress she wore, while most of the men went shirtless with jeans or cotton slacks with ties in the front. Most of the men wore either boots or running shoes while the women had on the same style of moccasin she'd found. Occasionally one of them would glance at the hut as though they knew she was there and she'd duck out of sight. But for the most part, they ignored her.

The sun dropped like a rock from the sky, plunging the world around them into darkness. The men started a large bonfire in the center of the area while the women went about cooking dinner over smaller campfires. A few women brought food from the cabins while others kept watch over the children. Laughter and the murmur of friendly talk flowed around her, making her wish she could join in. Her stomach rumbled, and although she'd found a bowl of fruit and a jug of water in a corner of the hut, she was still hungry. Would they bring her a meal once they'd finished eating?

Like a group of lifelong friends, the crowd passed around the food and drink, sharing whatever they had with everyone. A rotund man stood up and sang a song as the others feasted then roared their approval. Like a scene from a movie, they danced around the campfire, raising their cups in toasts and joking with their friends.

"Here."

She jumped, startled by Renkon's abrupt appearance. How had he snuck up on her?

He held out a metal plate filled with meat and potatoes along with cooked carrots and an apple. The large goblet he held in the other hand was filled with a dark liquid she guessed was wine. "Sorry, but I didn't know what you liked, so I brought a variety."

She couldn't help but return his infectious grin. His ocean-blue eyes sparkled with humor. "Thanks. Should I come out there?"

His smile faded. "No. For now, it's best that you stay inside. Rosh hasn't gained permission yet."

"Permission for what?"

"For you to join us."

Rosh's call had Renkon twisting his head around to nod at him. "Hold your horses. The girl has to eat."

Shay took the plate and drink. "Thanks. I'm Shay Mathews."

"I know. And I'm Rosh's better-looking cousin, Renkon McClain."

He could make her smile without trying. "Right. His better-looking, humble cousin."

"Now you've got it." He glanced back at Rosh. "Hang on, man."

"Would you like to sit with me?"

She'd surprised him as much as herself by offering.

"Sure." He held up a finger at a scowling Rosh then joined her inside the hut.

She drew in the aroma of the meal, but it was his scent that made her mouth water. Like Rosh, he smelled like steel, musk, and the forest around them. He was a man's man with broad shoulders she longed to run her hands over. He was tanned and rugged, and she dropped her gaze to her plate to keep from pushing him on his back and climbing on top of him as she'd done with Rosh.

"I'm sorry about how you came here."

She met his amazing eyes. "You are? But why? You're not the one who brought me."

"No, but I'm glad you're here."

The sizzle of powerful attraction she'd felt for Rosh came back, roaring between Renkon and her. "Why?"

His soft smile tore at her heart. She could sense a gentleness about him, one that was as appealing as the hardness Rosh had.

"Have you ever met anyone and just clicked?"

"I guess so. Maybe."

He skimmed his fingers along her leg, inching toward the hem of her dress. Yet as soon as he reached the material, he pulled his hand away. "No, if you had, there'd be no maybe about it."

She put her food down. Potatoes and the chicken were the last things she wanted to feast on. "I don't know what you're getting at."

"So you don't sense that we could have something like that?"

Her mouth parted and he lowered his gaze to her lips. The urge to kiss him swept through her with a dizzying effect. She was astonished that she resisted it. "I-I don't know."

A sad look crossed over his face. "I helped take care of you." He indicated the bed they sat on. "While you were healing."

"And?" What would he tell her? And yet, she couldn't imagine that he'd tell her anything she wouldn't like.

"You woke up once and we talked. Do you remember?"

"No." She wished she had.

"Well, we did. You told me about all sorts of things. About your life, your friends. We talked—okay, I did the most talking—for a while. You're special. I suspected it the second I laid eyes on you, but after that, I was sure."

He'd stolen her ability to speak. Yet when he touched her again, she believed him. Like Rosh, he was special, too. But just how special?

"Renkon, come on!"

He sighed. "Rosh is anything but patient. Especially about waiting on someone."

She grinned, at once disappointed and relieved that they couldn't speak longer.

"Don't worry. We won't take long. Until then, stick to the hut." He opened the flap and she followed part of the way out before he stopped her.

"Why? Because he hasn't gotten permission?"

A strange expression darkened his face as his gaze drifted to the woods behind the hut. "That and for other reasons." The smile was back in full force. "Gotta run."

"But wait." She didn't want him to leave. Instead, she would've liked to have spent more time with him. Maybe she could get a few answers. Or kiss him. Or more. But he was already halfway to Rosh before she could say anything more.

All at once, a strange, animallike wail drifted into the air, and everyone stopped what they were doing. As soon as the sound had faded, the women began gathering the children and hurrying them toward the cabins. The men grouped together and, as if on cue, tugged off their shoes and jeans.

She gaped at them. Most of them had good physiques although not as rugged as Rosh's, Renkon's, and Walker's. A few of them looked like the average office worker with his belly full from a weekend beer fest. Yet none of them acted embarrassed or shy. Instead, they treated each other no differently than when they'd worn clothing. The men turned toward the cabins as the doors opened and most of the women who'd gone inside came running out, pulling their dresses over their heads and tossing them to the ground. She assumed that the other women had stayed inside, closing the shutters on the cabins to keep the children from peeking out.

Had Rosh taken her to a nudist colony? Not that she was against that sort of thing, but these people seemed freer, even more comfortable in their own skin than any nudist. It was as if their nudity was not a choice but a necessity.

Men and women came together, arms entwining, legs wrapping around waists. She blinked, noting that each woman had at least two men with her. A few of them fell to the ground where they were, kissing and fondling one another. Two men positioned their woman between them, supporting her as one man shoved his cock inside her pussy while the other entered from behind.

"Holy shit." She'd heard of orgies, but she'd never seen one.

A blonde woman squirmed in feigned fear as the three men next to her grabbed her and dragged her inside a tent. A large woman, her heavy pendulum breasts resting against her full stomach, basked in the attention of two very fit, very handsome men. More and more of the women led their men inside a hut or a tent, but none took their men back to the cabins.

Her heart pounded as desire rushed outward from her pussy. Although voyeurism had never been her thing, she doubted anyone could keep from getting turned on by the scene. The men, although commanding and dominant, catered to their women, treating them with respect. Even when they handled their partner roughly, she could sense an underlying affection and adoration. The men were real men who treated their women like goddesses that they not only worshipped but hungered for.

Some of the men, including Rosh, Renkon, and Walker, who were not involved with the women strode away from the fire, blending into the darkness surrounding the campground. She wasn't sure if they'd gone into the woods or if they stood on the outskirts watching. Taking one last look at the sexual antics, she forced her mind back to the task she'd almost forgotten. Now was the time to make her getaway.

Checking to her right then to her left, she eased the flap back and slipped around the side of the hut. The tree line was several yards away and the area was dimly lit by the bonfire. Taking care to watch where she stepped, she ran as hard as she could to the trees then slipped under the low-hanging branches and into the forest.

Luck was with her as she came upon a dirt path that provided a break from the thick underbrush. She quickened her pace to match the quick beats of her heart. She hoped the path would lead to another campground or perhaps even a ranger station. She wasn't sure where she was or even what state she was in, but every forest had rangers, right?

Stumbling, she let out a yelp then got back on her feet. Time meant nothing in the darkness, and she had no idea how long she'd traveled. At last, she had to stop and rest.

Sinking to the ground, she pulled off her shoes and turned them over, dumping out pebbles and sticks that were biting into her feet. A sound to her left had her freezing like a deer hearing a nearby predator, but when she didn't hear the noise again, she let out a breath and calmed her nerves.

Take it easy. You can do this.

She glanced back the way she'd come. Would Rosh or Renkon come looking for her? She doubted it.

The sharp pang of disappointment deep in her gut surprised her. Why would she want them to? And yet, the memory of the way Rosh had held her, had cocooned her in his arms, came crashing back. The tender way Renkon had gazed at her left her wishing she could see that look one more time.

She wiped a tear from her cheek. She wasn't crying about them. That couldn't happen. She was just tired and a little scared. If she forced herself to think rationally and calmly, she'd realize that her emotions were out of whack from everything she'd gone through.

Should she try and find a place to hide and sleep through the night? Walking in the daytime would be safer and faster. Besides, she was exhausted and needed the sleep.

A different, louder noise not too far from her changed her mind. Pushing to her feet, she moved carefully but swiftly forward.

God, if you get me back safe and sound, I swear I'll never drive in the snow again.

God, if you get me back safe and sound, I swear I'll stay in Passion and never leave again.

God, if you get me back safe and sound, I swear I'll adopt ten orphans.

She pushed a branch out of the way.

Okay, maybe not that third one. Instead, I'll make a donation to the first church I see.

She paused to draw in a ragged breath. Was that running water? Was the waterfall nearby?

Listening as hard as she could, she tried to determine where the sound was coming from. At last, she headed off in a parallel direction, leaving the path to forge her way through the underbrush.

* * * *

Shay had taken his breath away the first time he'd seen her. Walker could still remember the intense sensation that swept over him as Rosh burst into the campground with her in his arms. Her body still glistened with drops of water as her arms hung limply by her sides. Her hair, a dark cascade trailing down to Rosh's thighs, swayed with his movements and her skin was tanned and glowing. Long, dark eyelashes feathered over her skin and a rose tint colored her pale cheeks. Her chest was large, but not overly so, and led his gaze to the swell of her stomach. Her legs were shapely and beckoned a man to caress them.

She was the most glorious vision he'd ever seen.

He'd followed Rosh toward the hut that he shared with his cousin Renkon. But Rosh had ignored his questions and refused him entrance to the hut. Fortunately, Renkon had relented whenever Rosh wasn't around and he'd gotten to spend time alone with her on two occasions. He'd stared at her and listened to her mutter in her sleep. His heart had leapt to his throat when she'd opened her eyes and looked up at him, but he couldn't tell if she'd really seen him.

Walker grumbled under his breath. Rosh and he had never called each other friends, but they'd managed to act civilly toward each other. They were, after all, part of The Hidden and, as such, they were expected to treat other with respect.

But their personalities had clashed from the moment Walker had entered The Hidden a year earlier after leaving his practice as a plastic surgeon in his hometown of Greensboro, North Carolina. He'd tried to get along with Rosh, but Rosh had remained hardheaded, preferring to spend his time with his cousin and a few select others. Yet, a year later, Walker was content living in his new home and had no intention of ever leaving.

Renkon and he got along well enough. Why couldn't he do the same with Rosh?

He studied Rosh. Maybe Charlton was right. Maybe it was because they were alphas who needed a pack to lead. Or maybe it was because they were among the strongest men in The Hidden. They were always fierce competitors in the games the men played and, on more than one occasion, Walker had bested Rosh in hunting. Was Rosh jealous? He doubted it. Maybe it really was as simple as being too much alike.

In a few rare moments, like after a successful run or when they'd shared in a celebration, they'd actually gotten along. But then they'd argue about who would lead a hunt or something equally trivial, and the barrier between them would go up again.

With Shay's arrival, he'd known that the time for them to put aside their differences had come. As stubborn as Rosh was, Walker vowed to find a way for them to live together as her mates. For their sakes as well as Shay's.

Walker saw Shay scurry around the hut and break into a trot toward the forest. He opened his mouth, ready to tell Rosh and Renkon, then closed it. They'd had their chance with her. He didn't know if they'd told her about both of them wanting her, but it didn't matter. He'd smelled her woman scent on Rosh. Now it was his turn.

He'd take this time to convince her that he should join Rosh and Renkon as one of her mates. If she agreed, Rosh and Renkon would have to accept her decision. That was the way of The Hidden.

He lifted the jug of wine he held and shook it. "We're almost out. I'll get some more." Without waiting for the cousins to respond, he headed for a cellar located in the basement of the nearest cabin. They'd managed to accumulate a large store of wine, champagne, beer, and other drinks by carrying the barrels and crates in from The Outside. The way was longer than jumping into the water, but that had been the only way to get supplies through to keep the community going.

Halfway to the cabin, he glanced over his shoulder, saw that they weren't watching him, then dashed behind the nearest tent. Leaving his cup and the jug there, he checked again, made sure that they were engrossed in the orgy, then ran toward the woods.

It wasn't long until he'd caught up with her. Yet instead of grabbing her and hauling her back, he hung behind, keeping guard, knowing that he risked much in doing so. But with the greatest risks came the greatest rewards.

Had Rosh told her about The Cursed yet? If so, why would she risk going into the forest at night? He should take her back before anything happened, but he was too curious and too determined to make his case. Where did she think she was going anyway? No one could find their way out of The Hidden on their own even when The Time of Leaving was present.

Although The Cursed could venture out in the day, they preferred the cover darkness gave them. Night was when they went hunting for food. But animals weren't their only prey. They snuck through the trees in search of anyone unlucky or foolish enough to venture away from their home. He had no doubt that Shay would make one or more of them a grand prize. His inner wolf growled at the idea of one of them touching her, and he swore he'd die before he let that happen.

He stayed behind the trees, staying even with her as she hurried down the path. When she almost fell a couple of times, he wanted to reach out and catch her.

She cried out in joy when she broke through the trees and found the small pond. The majestic waterfall, a different one than the one they used to enter The Hidden, rose high above the clear blue-green water until the top of it could barely be seen in the low-lying clouds. She stood, her head thrown back to survey the water as it plunged over the precipice of the cliff and fell to form a curtain of white foam.

Her hair streamed over her shoulders, lifting with a slight breeze. Her profile was that of a queen, serene yet powerful. She thrust out her chest as she fisted her hands on her hips like an explorer claiming victory in her discovery. The dress she wore molded to the rounded curves of her body as the mist floated to wet the simple material. His heart swelled with pride. His woman-to-be was all woman, proud of her voluptuous form and strong in spirit. From what he'd heard Rosh and Renkon speak of her, she was also intelligent and witty.

She would be his. Sooner or later. To think otherwise would be to doom his existence.

His cock twitched, aching to break free of his jeans, when she pulled up the hem of her dress and walked into the shallow water. He wished he was the cool liquid that flowed around her body, over her skin, and between her legs. The swell of her sweet ass led to the material floating away from her, and he held his breath as the water rose around her shapely breasts.

Was she chilled? Were her nipples hard? Had the temperature of the pond vanquished the heat of her pussy? He doubted any cold could ever smother that fire.

Her hair spread out as she leaned back and pushed off the bottom then swam toward the falling water. He shucked his boots and jeans, realizing that she thought an exit lay behind the liquid curtain and knowing that she was wrong.

The moment she pushed her way to the small area behind the curtain, he waded into the pond then ducked underneath and breaststroked his way to her. She was sitting on the slender ledge that ran from one side of the fall to the other when he broke through the surface. Startled, she pulled her legs out of the water and hugged them to her chest.

Drops slid down her face, over the material that was stuck to her breasts. Her taut nipples looked like hard points of delight, and, if she hadn't drawn up her legs, he would've guessed that he could see her patch of curly dark hair pressed against the wet dress. She'd sleeked her hair away from her face, letting the moisture from it trickle around her shoulders.

"Shay."

She gasped, then recovered and jutted out her chin. "You know me? I saw you with Rosh. It's Walker, right?"

He was encouraged that she knew his name. "Yeah. Walker Ramirez. I'm, uh, friends with Rosh and Renkon."

She scoffed. "It didn't look like you and Rosh were friends."

He treaded water and kept his attention on her beautiful face. If he let it drop lower, he'd find it very hard to concentrate. "We have our moments."

"Why do you look familiar?" Her dark eyes zeroed in on him and her tone held a note of suspicion. "Have we met?"

"Yes and no."

"What does that mean?"

He laughed and grabbed hold of the ledge. "You were in and out of it while you were healing. Once or twice I thought you opened your eyes, but I wasn't sure you saw me."

"How did you know I was here?"

Hadn't she heard him the few times that he'd made a noise, intending to keep her wary of her surroundings? "I saw you leave and followed you."

She frowned, making a face that on any other woman would've been ugly. "So you were stalking me?"

He liked the way she voiced whatever was on her mind. "Not

exactly. I was making sure you didn't get hurt."

"Uh-huh. Well, as you can see, I'm fine. So go on back to the camp. You wouldn't want to miss the orgy."

He pulled his body onto the ledge, making her draw her knees closer to her chest. "I don't care about that."

"If you're trying to tell me that you're gay, I'm not buying it." Her gaze dropped to his crotch.

He glanced down at his fully erect penis. "That's not at all what I'm saying. I've never participated in the lovemaking, because it would be just a physical thing. I didn't have the right woman." He brought his gaze to hers, pushing all he was feeling into his look. "Until now."

She didn't act surprised, other than giving a quick jerk of her head. Did that mean she was open to the idea?

"What's with you guys anyway? What's going on? Every time I ask Rosh, he gets cut off."

He eased closer. The warmth from her body wafted off her and over him. She was hot for him. Why else would she keep dropping her gaze to his cock? "I'm not sure what you mean."

"Oh, come on. I crash my car because some *thing* rushes into the middle of the road. Then, not being of sound mind and body, I think I can go toe-to-toe with a huge wolf. I conk out and come to with Rosh treating me like a sack of flour. Then he tosses me over a waterfall, and I wake up days later living in a strange, primitive Shangri-La. This is like a story from *The Twilight Zone*, so don't tell me you don't know what I mean."

Damn, but he loved the way her eyes blazed and her mouth twisted to the side as she paused in her tirade to take a quick breath. He reached up and took a strand of her wet hair. She tensed but didn't pull away.

"You're the most beautiful woman I've ever seen."

She tugged her hair away. "Don't try and change the subject. I'm tired of you macho men ordering me around and not telling me what I want to know. So get with it. Spill, buddy, or I'm kicking you off this ledge." She pointed her finger at him. "And don't think I won't do it, either. Once I set my mind on something—"

He cocooned her finger in his hand. "Shay, will you be quiet for a second and listen to me?"

She slammed her mouth shut then arched an eyebrow, giving him what he'd asked for. Or at least he thought so.

"Hell, no. Not until you tell me what the fuck—"

He did the only thing he could do. He stopped her talking by crushing his mouth to hers. Amazingly, she still tried to speak, but he cupped her neck and kept the kiss going. She could struggle all she wanted, but he wouldn't let her go.

Her knees pushed against his chest, getting in his way, so he took an ankle and yanked her leg straight. Her other leg fell to the side, giving him the opening he needed. He slid closer, putting his body between her legs. His cock rubbed against her inner thigh, and she gasped but didn't move away.

He slid his hand to the curve of her neck, hooked his thumb under the top of the dress, and pushed the sleeve down her shoulder. He broke the kiss, keeping his hand behind her neck as he sought out her eyes. The chocolate brown in them had deepened and her pupils had grown bigger. She wanted him, her body recognizing his need as well as hers, and, if she didn't screw it up by letting her mind take over, he'd get his chance to show her how much he needed her.

He kissed the corner of her slightly parted lips then feathered more kisses along her cheek and down to her collarbone. The hollow above her shoulder blade turned him on even more as he took a quick bite. She arched her back, thrusting her breasts toward him.

"Lie back."

She did so without questioning him, and he had to grit back a grin. Tugging the other sleeve down, he exposed her breasts and almost lost control. His inner wolf howled and pranced, urging him to take her before she changed her mind.

"God, you're beautiful."

"You already said that," she whispered.

He did grin then. "And I'll say it a million times more."

She looked shocked, as though she believed him. And why shouldn't she? He'd spoken the truth. If she hadn't heard it in his voice, then she could see it in his eyes.

He caressed her breasts, holding them like long-sought-after treasure. Putting one to his cheek, he closed his eyes, drew in her sweet scent, and rubbed the stubble on his cheek over the soft surface.

He took her nipple, sucking off the remnants of her swim. Pulling it into his mouth, he bit down and moved his jaw back and forth to torture the taut bud. She moved her legs restlessly but didn't wrap them around his waist.

Disappointment flooded him, but he pushed it away. He had their instinctive pull toward each other to thank for getting as far as he had. But that didn't mean he couldn't make her want to go further.

He knew she was the one for him. Werewolves almost always recognized their mate as soon as they met her. Yet, unlike when werewolves were on The Outside, they didn't get an energy or physical bond that pulled them together while in The Hidden. Perhaps it wasn't needed in The Hidden since the place held a magic of its own. As far as he was concerned it didn't matter.

Instead, it was the opposite. Being with another woman who they found attractive, who they hoped might be their mate but wasn't, left an emptiness in them that no amount of courtship or knowledge could fill. They could learn everything about a woman, her likes, her dislikes, how caring or giving she was. They could even grow to care for her, but that hole, the realization that they were missing an ingredient that would make their world complete, never went away. Not until they found the right woman.

Could she sense that she belonged with him? Maybe with Rosh and Renkon, too? The males wanted to share a woman, finding monogamy a chain that fostered infidelity and a loss of their freedom.

While the men needed only one woman to come home to, a woman, especially a woman in The Hidden, needed more than one man. No one man could give her everything she needed, and, realizing that, the werewolves of The Hidden were eager to share. Mating a woman to at least one other man gave the men what they wanted most. By making their mate happy and contented, they served their purpose in life.

He was about to burst, both emotionally and physically. But he had to make sure that he gave to her first. Before he would allow himself to release, he'd make sure that he fulfilled her pleasure. He peered at her from behind lowered eyelids and pushed his body lower.

Her mouth parted as she realized what he was about to do. "Walker."

"Trust me, Shay. Close off your thoughts and listen to your heart." He stopped her, unable to hear her tell him to go. When she didn't say anything else, he settled at her vee, pushed the dress higher to expose her, then positioned her legs over his shoulders.

Her sweet aroma swept over him as he placed his face close to her pussy lips. No other woman had her special fragrance. No other woman's pussy was as beautiful. Yet instead of professing to her again how stunning she was, he let his actions show her.

She settled back and clutched her breasts. Her legs trembled, and he hadn't even touched her pussy yet.

Easing out his tongue, he lightly skimmed the tip over the crease of her labia. She jerked then stilled and let out a soft moan. Moving closer, he kissed the tender skin between her leg and her pussy and smiled as she once again startled. She was like a virgin, quick to bolt, but he knew she had the experience of a woman.

Tenderly, reverently, he pulled her lips apart and took his first look at her pink treasure. It glistened with her wetness. Reaching out again with his tongue, he flicked it over her tender bundle of nerves. This time, she didn't buck but instead pushed her pelvis toward him, urging him to give her what she so badly wanted.

He couldn't have waited any longer anyway. Taking hold of her ample bottom, he put his mouth against her and took in his first drink. His lust soared to a new height as he pulled her clit into his mouth then sucked harder to bring in every drop he could. His fingers dug into her ass, harder than he'd thought to do so, but she didn't complain. She could take everything he had to give her and more.

"Walker."

Damn, how he loved the way she said his name. He answered, but the word was muffled. He lashed at her hard nub with his tongue, first fast and hard then slowly as he made circles around it.

A breeze swept over them, blowing mist from the waterfall onto her body. He could see the water beading on her rounded stomach and the goose bumps along her arms.

He drank from her then added first one, then another finger to her pussy. She moaned and reached out for him, but he was too low for her to touch. Taking it easy at first, he darted his gaze between his fingers sliding in and out to the ecstasy of her expression.

Her eyes were clouded with lust, and his cock ached to take the place of his fingers. But she came first.

Rocking back and forth, she clenched her vaginal walls around his fingers. He groaned, thinking about how good she'd feel wrapped around his cock. She was tight, and his shaft would stretch her to the limit, but he had no doubt she'd hold on to him until she'd dragged out every drop of his seed.

A warm gush of moisture flowed over his fingers, and he pulled them out to press his mouth to her pussy then stick his tongue inside her as far as he could. She tasted even sweeter than before, her climax giving her another flavor that he'd forever recognize as hers.

She bucked against him, away from him, but he held on. Torturing her, he sucked harder and massaged her clit with his tongue. He took her from the first orgasm through the delightful, painful journey as her body readied for an even bigger release. She shouted, the cry turning into a groan as her next climax tore through her.

"Shay! Where are you?"

Damn it!

In the next moment, Walker found himself yanked off the ledge. He went under the water, kicking at whoever held his leg.

* * * *

Shay sat up, pulling her dress hem down and the top up to cover her breasts. Walker resurfaced, sputtering curses. Renkon burst out from the water beside him, and, a few moments later, Rosh broke through, gripped the rock, and pulled his body next to hers.

"Are you all right?" His dark eyes scanned her.

"She was until you two showed up." Walker scowled at Rosh then got back on the ledge on the other side of her.

Although the water was chilly, their body heat wrapped around her, warming her then sinking into her skin to send thrills to her already-throbbing pussy. "Did the whole damn camp follow me?"

She narrowed her eyes and put on an angry expression, but the truth of it was that she was not only flattered, but excited that all three men had wanted to find her. Yet, now that she'd gotten intimate with Walker, would Renkon and Rosh think less of her? She wasn't the kind of girl who had sex right after meeting a man. That wasn't her style, and yet, she'd done exactly that twice now.

But she wasn't ashamed. She couldn't explain it, but she felt as though she already knew them. Like lovers from a different lifetime who had found each other again.

Sheesh! I can't believe that even makes sense. When did I become a romantic?

Renkon chuckled then skimmed his fingers along her foot. "Why would they do that?"

"Why would *you* do that?" She pulled away even though his touch echoed that of his cousin's and Walker's.

All three men tilted their heads to stare at her. Their looks matched, and she watched their eyes darken.

Holy hell, but they make me want to do naughty things. She trembled, but she didn't feel chilled.

"To keep your pretty little ass safe, that's why."

Her first reaction was to chew Rosh's butt off until what he'd said hit her. Pretty *little* ass? Was the man blind? She resisted the urge to glance at her backside. Had she somehow gotten smaller without knowing it?

Okay. It's impossible, but he just got even sexier.

"You promised you wouldn't try to run off again."

Aw, shit. Then he has to go and blow it.

Shay shoved both Rosh's and Walker's hands away as they each tried to take one of her arms. Having them touch her would only make it difficult to think. She tried to cast her gaze somewhere else so she could listen to her head and not her libido, but she was surrounded by sexy, hard bodies. Maybe she should calm down and reconsider her options. After all, how many times did such a tantalizing opportunity come along? Three men, one woman, all of them hot and wet. What more could she ask for?

"Yeah, well, I lied. So sue me."

"Watch out. He just might." Renkon shrugged his shoulders at Rosh's scowl. "What? Like you're never going to tell her that you're an attorney? An assistant district attorney, to be exact. Me? I'm just an unemployed lover of life."

"I was an attorney, but I'm not a lawyer any longer. We have no use for such things here. Just like we have no use for a former plastic surgeon like Walker."

An attorney and a plastic surgeon? Why would two high-power men come to live in the forest?

"So you three came here to live? Or do you travel back and forth?"

"That would make for one hell of a commute." Renkon chuckled and even Walker and Rosh exchanged smiles.

"Wow. But that brings up my other questions. Questions you

promised to answer but haven't."

She pivoted to confront Rosh and almost forgot what she was going to say when he leaned forward and put his face a few inches from hers. "I, uh, I want to know where I am, how I got here, and how I get back to my car. Or to any place where there are civilized people who don't frolic naked in the woods and have orgies by a bonfire."

"Did you like what you saw?"

She whipped her attention back to Walker. Was he talking about the orgy? Or the fact that she had three very hot, lust-filled, naked men next to her? Even submerged up to his shoulders, she could see through the clear water to know that Renkon's cock could match the other men's with no problem.

Pussy to head. Take back control, please.

"You know what he's talking about, Shay. The lovemaking back at camp. I can't wait until we can take part in it with you." Renkon pulled himself up by clinging to the edge but kept his lower half in the water. He grabbed her foot and caressed it then brought it to his mouth and sucked on her big toe. He lashed his tongue between her toes, nibbling on the ends of them, then drew in her big toe again.

She inhaled and knew she should take it away, but couldn't. Instead, she watched, fascinated, as he flicked his tongue around the tip of her toe.

She'd never cared much about having so much attention paid to her feet, but Renkon could easily change her mind. The sensation of his tongue on her skin was wiping everything else out of her mind. "I'm getting confused. I–I can't think."

"Don't try. Just feel." Rosh cupped her breast and kissed her on the neck. His bites traveled up until he found her earlobe and started nibbling.

Her body relaxed, and she vaguely wondered if they'd put a spell on her. Her questions no longer mattered. The only important thing was to get closer to them. She moaned as Walker took her other breast and massaged her nipple with his thumb. Their touches were so wonderful that it was as if she no longer wore the dress.

"Don't leave me out of this." Renkon shifted her toward him then eased his hand between her legs. He found her curly patch of hair and pressed his palm against her mons. Going in a slow, easy circle, he put pressure on her, and once again her body reacted with a swift and urgent release.

She closed her eyes and rested against the wall. Answers could come later. She couldn't turn them away, not when her body called for them, ached to have their tongues, their fingers, their bodies on her.

"Back off, Walker."

She opened her eyes, bereft of Walker's and Rosh's hands and mouths. Renkon took his hand away, grumbling that they were screwing things up. But the two men ignored him, their glares heated, their jaws set.

"That's for her to decide," ground out Walker. "You know that's our way. You can't tell me to leave. Not now. Not ever, if that's what she wants."

Rosh rose to squat on the narrow ledge. "I brought her here, and that makes her my responsibility. That makes me the first one she'll choose. Then Renkon. If she wants another, then she can make that decision after she answers us."

"Fine with me because I know she'll choose me, too." Walker closed his eyes a moment as though trying to regroup before opening them again. "Come on, man. Give it a rest between us."

"Hey, hold up." She pressed her palms against their hard chests. "I don't have a clue what you're going on about. Choose who? For what? For sex? Because if that's it, then, yeah, I'm the one who says who I want and don't want. Or even *if* I want."

Yeah, right. Like I'm going to turn them away.

"If you three don't want to play nice, then you'll have to learn what any kindergartener knows. You'll have to learn to take turns and share."

She dragged in a breath. Had she just promised to have sex with them? Separate or together? When had she become so promiscuous? Yet they made the decision easy. She took a good look at each of them in turn. Other than Rosh having a problem with Walker, they seemed to like the idea.

Hell, yeah, I'll have them. I'd be crazy not to. But only on my terms.

She tried to focus. How had they gotten off track again? She needed answers, and she needed a guide to take her home. "Look, guys. We're going to have to shelve this discussion for later. Rosh, I understand that you thought you were saving me and everything, and truthfully, this whole adventure has been really fun. Aside from the whole throwing-me-over-the-cliff thing. But let's get down to business. Which one of you is going to take me back to Montana?"

Renkon shook his head. "Shay, babe, you're still in Montana. We're not even that far from where you met Rosh."

"Like hell I am. It's winter and cold and snowy in Montana and—"

A growl filtered through the wall of water. More growls echoed the first.

Rosh clamped a hand over her mouth as Walker and Renkon twisted toward the pond beyond. She squinted and took Rosh's hand away, nodding that she'd stay quiet.

Another growl rent the air.

Renkon dove under, lengthening his form as he kicked his feet and tunneled his fingers through the water. Rosh tensed then nodded at Walker as though acknowledging a silent message before diving after his cousin.

Walker took her hand and held it firmly. "Listen to me. You have to do exactly what I tell you to do."

The intensity in his eyes kept her silent as tension crawled into her neck. She inclined her head and waited for him to go on.

"There are things out there, like the one you saw on the road. They're dangerous, vicious, and willing to do almost anything to find a human woman to take as their own."

"A human woman?" *As opposed to what? An inhuman one?*

"I can't explain it right now. There's no time."

A series of growls erupted, sounding as though they were all around them. She narrowed her eyes, trying to see past the waterfall. "What are they?"

"Again. Later." He took her face in his hands and made her look at him. "Stay close to me. No matter what happens, no matter what you see, do not leave my side. And above all else, don't get out of the water until at least one of us or our friends comes for you."

"I don't understand. If these things are that dangerous, why doesn't someone call the police?"

"We handle our own problems here." He tried to hide the wince he made as yet another series of growls came. "Tell me you understand."

"I understand. I need to stick next to you and stay wet. Got it."

"Good. Follow me." He took her hand again and eased into the water. He helped her down, and she paddled her feet and held on to his shoulder. "Don't be afraid. We won't let them take you."

Take me? Oh, my God.

He winked at her then kissed her cheek, an obvious attempt to ease her fear. Then, with a solemn expression, he sank beneath the surface. She took a deep breath and slipped under to find him waiting for her. Pivoting toward the falls, he led her under the pounding water and into the pond.

Chapter Five

Shay shook her head then ran her fingers through her hair to get it out of her face. She wiped the dripping water away from her eyes then gaped at the shore, not believing what she saw.

Two large, black wolves paced the ground where the men's clothing lay. Their amber eyes flamed with challenge as they pulled their lips back into snarls, exposing sharp fangs. Closer to the tree line, six black forms bent over, their long arms grazing the leaves like great apes. Their skeletal bodies appeared almost human, yet each sported a straight, furless tail.

But it was their faces that fired panic in her heart. Reminding her of the popular drawings of aliens, they were oval-shaped with two holes bored into the flesh serving as nostrils. They had no hair and no fur. Pointed ears stuck out from their heads while red, soulless eyes glittered with evil ferocity, completing their otherworldly appearance. She lowered her gaze from those awful eyes and wished she hadn't. Each of them sported a huge, thick black cock.

One larger monster stood apart from the others. He appeared to be directing his friends with short barks of a language she couldn't understand. His slitted eyes locked on to hers, and she shivered. "Is that their leader?"

"Yeah. He's called Burac. He's smarter, faster, meaner than the others, and he's the only one who can speak any English. They have their own language, but we've yet to learn it."

She had to break eye contact with Burac. He had a terrifying allure about him, a siren's call that, if she wasn't careful, could take her over with its cold, dark spell. She forced her eyes closed and turned her head away from him then opened them to focus on Walker.

"His eyes. It's like he can see into my soul and yank it out."

Walker, treading water beside her, pulled her closer when she let out a small cry of dismay. "It's okay, I'm here. But try not to look at him. He has power and won't hesitate to use it."

"Why aren't they coming for us? They outnumber us."

"They hate water and won't risk getting wet. Not even Burac. You're safe here. Try to swim in the middle for as long as you can, but if we have to, you can stand in the shallow part."

"Can't we go back behind the waterfall?"

"No. We need to stay out in the open and keep them exposed, too. They could sneak up on us if we're on the ledge."

"But where are Renkon and Rosh? Did they go for help? Those things didn't get them, did they?" She didn't know them well, and yet she knew that they would never have deserted her.

But she didn't see their bodies. Had the creatures dragged them away? An ache was like a splinter in her heart. Could she have lost them?

"No, they're fine."

"Then where are they? I know they wouldn't run off and leave us. "And where did the wolves come from?"

Walker brought her legs around his waist, giving her time to rest. She clung to his neck as the creatures skittered back and forth in front of the wolves. "Rosh hasn't told you yet."

"He hasn't told me what?" Her heart leapt to her throat as one of the beasts jumped at the larger wolf. The wolf caught it in midair and, with a great shake of his head, tossed it back at the others. Its scream made her skin crawl.

"We have so much to explain to you."

"Just tell me where they are. Those…things…didn't get them, did they?"

"Shay, the wolves? That's Rosh and Renkon."

Rosh and Renkon are the wolves? "That's insane. How can that be?"

"Baby, they're werewolves."

At that moment, the largest wolf twisted around to look at her. His blazing eyes bored into her, but for a moment, she thought she saw a plea for understanding in them. "Werewolves? Like in the movies? That's ridiculous. Werewolves aren't real." Yet how else could she explain what she was seeing?

"Are those other things real?"

She studied the creatures stalking in front of the wolves. Could they be a species of animal that no one knew existed? Even if that were true, she could see that they possessed cunning and intelligence. They were monsters, and they were real. And if they were real, why couldn't werewolves be real?

The wolves were extraordinarily large with eyes unlike any other wolf's. They moved with deliberate steps, each never going too far from the other. Yet it was that pleading look that convinced her.

"Where am I? What is this place?" she whispered, awed by the realization that the world around her was not the same world she'd grown up in.

Before Walker could answer, howls and snarls bellowed, raising a horrible din. Three wolves, a buck, two brown bears, and a coyote emerged from the forest, jumping on top of the terrible creatures. The wolves—*Rosh and Renkon!*—joined in the battle that didn't last long. As soon as they could break free, the things rushed into the woods and disappeared. A few of the other animals followed, but most chased them only as far as the tree line.

Rosh and Renkon skirted the group and faced her. Shaking their heads, they began to change.

"Watch, Shay. But remember. They're still the same men underneath their fur."

As the rest of the animals drifted back into the darkness, the two wolves' bodies blurred. Cracking sounds coincided with the emergence of human limbs, and smooth human skin flowed over their bodies to replace the black fur. They put their backs to her as they twisted their bodies and the transformation continued. Pointed ears disappeared as rounded human ones replaced them. She wondered what their faces would look like as they regained their masculine shape, but they kept them averted.

She squinted, trying to see better, thinking that if she could make her brain believe what her eyes told her, she'd understand. Walker turned her loose then took her hand, and together, they swam toward the shore.

"You have nothing to fear from them. They'd die before they ever let any harm come to you. And I'd do the same."

She stood in shallow water, her pulse pounding a quick rhythm in her ears. Since awakening from her crash, the world hadn't been the same, but she hadn't thought it had changed that much. She'd come to a primitive yet amazing place. A place that she'd come to think of as odd but not entirely different from the rest of the world. But she'd gotten it wrong. The men she'd met, the men she was attracted to in every sense of the word, were the stuff fairy tales and monster movies were made of. Rosh and Renkon were werewolves.

Although she let Walker lead her closer to the shore, she wouldn't come out of the water. Walker didn't force her to follow him as he came to stand beside the other two men.

"Am I hallucinating? Or did I die in the crash and end up in another world? Maybe I'm in a coma and freaking out."

Rosh started to enter the water, but she shook her head and backed up. "It's okay, Shay. We'd never hurt you. Not as men and not as wolves."

"This is crazy. It's the gash on my head. It's making me see and hear strange things."

"What gash, Shay?"

She touched her forehead, only now remembering that the gash had healed quicker than she'd have thought possible. "I'm imagining that, too. That's got to be it. Those creatures and werewolves don't exist."

Renkon joined his cousin. "We're as real as you are. You'll realize that lots of things are real once you open your mind as well as your eyes. Just because you didn't know it before doesn't make them any less real."

She searched Walker. "Are you a werewolf, too?"

Walker held out his hand. "Trust us, baby. Come back with us and we'll explain everything."

Rosh twisted around to glare at him. "This isn't the way she was supposed to find out."

"But it's the way she did. You should've told her from the beginning. If you had, maybe she wouldn't have run off and almost gotten abducted by Burac and his kind."

Almost at once, Rosh lost his animosity. "You're right. And I'm glad you were here to help her."

Walker appeared surprised at Rosh's sudden shift in attitude. "You're the ones who fought them off."

"We want the same thing. For her to stay safe and be happy."

Walker nodded. "We do. That's all I'm asking for."

The two men regarded each other for a moment as though an unspoken truce had been reached. They shifted their attention back to her.

Her head spun with questions even as she tried to think clearly. If what she was seeing was true, didn't she want to know the how and why of it? But if she was imagining everything, why not continue the dream until she could wake up? In either case, her curiosity got the better of her. What other amazing sights would she see? Besides, she couldn't stay waist deep in water until she either woke up or figured out that another magical world existed. What if Burac and the others came back? Real or not, she didn't want to risk that.

"Shay, are you coming with us?"

She'd almost responded to Renkon's question when the idea hit her. "Why can't you take me back to my car? Unless I dreamed the accident, too."

"We can't. It's one of the rules of The Hidden." Rosh spread his arms wide, indicating the world around them. "Those who can come and go can only do so at specific times. Until then, you have to stay."

"That's what you call this world? The Hidden?"

"That's right, and the world you know is what we call The Outside. Those things are called The Cursed."

"So it's not that you won't show me the way out. It's that you can't. How convenient." She wanted to take back the words when she saw the hurt on their faces. Instead, she held her head high and walked toward the shore.

"Then you're coming back with us?"

The hope, the excitement in Renkon's tone was unmistakable.

"For now. But I want to know everything. Don't you dare leave any detail out. Now put on your clothes and let's get going." She pushed them away from her as they tried to take her arms, her hands. Gathering her nerve, she marched into the forest and prayed that no monsters waited in the underbrush.

* * * *

The four of them remained quiet as they hurried back to the camp. Renkon didn't know what his cousin or Walker intended to say, but he was ready to tell her everything if for no other reason than to keep her safe. Maybe if she'd known about The Cursed, she wouldn't have gone into the forest, especially at night. And now that she'd seen them in their wolf forms, what else was there to keep from her?

He cringed inwardly as the answer came. She still didn't realize that they wanted her as their mate. Whether that meant Rosh and he would share her, or if she'd want Walker in the relationship didn't matter to him. As long as he had her, he'd accept anything she wanted.

He glanced at the other two men who flanked her as he brought up the rear. He loved his cousin, and he liked Walker well enough. But could they get along? They often got on each other's nerves, but when things had gotten serious with The Cursed's attempt to take Shay, they'd come together. Had they come to an agreement afterward? Could she be the glue that would bind them together?

He lowered his gaze and smiled. Her round bottom was what most men would call a big booty, but it was perfect for him. Society outside The Hidden would never have called her beautiful. She wasn't skinny, blonde, or tall. But he loved the shape of her body. She had curves and valleys that he wanted to explore for the rest of his life. He was glad that werewolves lived longer than humans, and if she agreed to the change, she'd live as long as they did.

He wouldn't have believed that he could fall for someone so fast, but he had. At first, he'd thought Rosh had made a huge mistake in bringing her into The Hidden. Then to state that they both wanted her for their mate? He'd understood that Rosh had said so to keep The Council from sending her back, but at the time, he'd thought Rosh insane for sticking his neck out for a stranger. Yet when he'd entered their hut and seen her, he'd quickly understood. No one, especially not his cousin and him, would want to see her harmed.

At first, he'd still tried to deny it, to chalk his feelings up to simple sexual attraction, but the longer he gazed on her beautiful face, so pale while she was recuperating, the more he grew to want to know her, to wonder what her laugh would sound like, to yearn to touch her.

Soon, he'd have to tell her how he felt. He'd taken his time while Rosh and then Walker enjoyed her, but that was his way. Where his cousin was brash and ready to leap into action, he was careful, considering his moves before doing anything.

Taking care of her had opened a warm place in his heart that he hadn't known existed. The way she'd moaned while tossing in her sleep, seeing her smooth forehead marred with lines as she dreamed had made him want to soothe and comfort her. And when she'd opened her eyes and yet hadn't really seen him, it didn't matter. He'd gazed deeply into hers and had known, right then and there, that he'd do anything to keep her safe.

At first reticent about helping to care for her, he'd soon found himself spending more and more time in the hut. He and his cousin had talked of taking turns watching her, but soon that idea vanished and they'd both found themselves taking care. He could still remember the way her pink lips parted when he'd lifted her head and urged her to drink. He could still see the rise and fall of her chest that made his cock harden while his heart softened.

He'd found his cousin and had questioned him at length about her. The way Rosh spoke of her, how she'd tried to protect what she'd thought was a helpless fawn, told him of her compassion. But she had courage, too. Not only was she willing to fight the wolf about to attack the fawn, she was brave—albeit foolish—enough to try to run off on her own. He'd always hoped that his mate would have both empathy and courage.

He smiled, his gaze still fixed on her bottom. It didn't hurt that she'd given Rosh a run for his money, struggling against him as he'd carried her through the forest then thrown her over the cliff and into the waterfall. He wished he could have seen that.

She was everything he'd dreamed of and more. She'd wrapped him in a spell as surely as if she were a witch.

Hating to do so, he forced his mind away from her apple bottom, away from the seductive sway of her hips, and away from her hair that swung back and forth. He had to keep watch in case Burac decided to try again.

He breathed a sigh of relief once they reentered the camp. Their friends had already returned home, and the camp was buzzing with the news of Burac's attempt to snatch Shay. The women surrounded her, making sure she was all right.

Myla, a shape-shifter and Kira's mother, offered her a soothing drink then turned to the men and scowled. Her bright green eyes could've turned them to stone if she'd had Medusa's power. Her curly red hair stood out from her head as though the fury she felt sent energy to the tips of her locks. Her petite frame, her height being less than five feet, might've tricked a man into thinking she was timid and even demure, but Renkon had witnessed her temper too many times to be fooled by her size.

Renkon stayed behind Rosh and Walker. Myla's temper was legendary, and he had no wish to catch the full brunt of it.

"What are you men doing? Why haven't you told her about us? About you?" She pushed against Rosh's chest and sent him stumbling backward.

"I was going to."

"Bullshit. That's an excuse and you know it. It's bad enough that she was brought here against her will, but to keep her in the dark about the world around her is nothing short of irresponsible."

"I brought her here to save her life. She knows that."

"Well, obviously she either doesn't care or didn't understand. Otherwise, she wouldn't have taken off in the middle of the night. What if they'd gotten her? What then?"

Rosh backed up again when Myla took another step toward him. Walker played it safe and moved closer to Renkon, out of the line of fire. "I get it, Myla, I screwed up. But let's remember how this all got started. If you hadn't let Kira go off into the woods by herself, I wouldn't have had to chase after her and get involved."

Myla crossed her arms over her chest and lowered her chin to stare up at him with hooded eyes. "And you'd have never met her, either. Remember that. And remember this, too, you flea-ridden hound, I asked you to fetch my daughter, not to play a game of chase. But none of that means anything. You should've told her the first chance you got, and you didn't."

Rosh finally held up his hands, admitting the defeat everyone else had known was inevitable. "You're right. But don't worry. We're explaining everything tonight."

"See that you do." Myla whirled to face the crowd of women

surrounding Shay. "Let her be now. She needs to go with her men."

Her men. That sounds damn good. Renkon couldn't hold back his smile. "Come with us into the hut, Shay. We have a lot to tell you."

Shay thanked the women, and, letting Rosh lead the way, she followed Walker and Renkon into the hut. Renkon cast a grin at Myla, winked, then hurried inside when her scowl grew bigger.

Shay sat cross-legged in the middle of their bed. Her dark hair floated around her shoulders and her clasped hands pushed the dress in between her legs. Need washed over Renkon, and with one look, he knew the other two men felt the same way. If they had their way, she'd have already disrobed and stretched out on her back, her arms spread wide to welcome them.

He settled next to Rosh and across from Walker. A dim light seeped through the opening above while candles that the women had lit in preparation for her safe return cast their shadows on the walls. If she said yes, if she accepted her new life with them, they'd have to get a larger dwelling. Although they preferred sleeping close to the ground, they'd build her a cabin of her own if she wanted. Hopefully, he'd help her fill it with lots of children.

"Okay, I'm listening. Start talking. Tell me that you and Renkon are really werewolves."

They'd known she had spirit and had discussed how much they loved that about her. But her spirit could mean that she might be difficult to handle, and she'd shown them that it was true. Still, he wouldn't have asked her to change.

Rosh started them off, and Renkon could only trust that he wouldn't get angry if she didn't react the way he thought she should. His cousin kept his head down, his attention on the bed, before finally lifting his head. His expression was solemn, and Renkon could sense his nervousness. If she didn't agree to stay, they'd be lost forever, loveless and alone. He doubted that he could remain in The Hidden if she wasn't there with him.

"Let me start from the beginning. It'll make more sense that way."

Rosh dragged in a long breath. "When I found you that day—"

"I think it was the other way around. I sort of found you and whacked you over the head."

Renkon rolled his lips under to keep from chuckling. She was feisty and ready to speak her mind. Life with her wouldn't be dull.

To Rosh's credit, he let her interruption slide. "Anyway, you had a gash on your head and a car that wasn't going to take you anywhere. Then, after you 'whacked me over the head' as you put it, you passed out. I could've left you there in the snow or put you back in the car. Either way I doubt you would've survived. At least not without losing a few fingers and toes from frostbite. The only other option was to bring you here."

"No. You could've taken me down the mountain or phoned for help."

Renkon shook his head along with Rosh. "Not true. If you'll remember, I didn't have a phone on me. Plus, I wasn't about to walk into a gas station or anywhere else buck naked, carrying an unknown injured woman. No, my only option was to bring you to The Hidden."

"The Hidden. What does that mean anyway? Hidden from what?" She leaned forward, her expression frustrated, yet curious.

Rosh paused, and Walker took the chance to answer. "The Hidden is a place where people like us can come and let our true natures show. Not many on The Outside, in the world you know, are aware of The Hidden."

"But I don't get it. How can you keep a place like this unknown? It's not like we're in the middle of Africa or on the moon." She paused, hopping her gaze from Walker, to Rosh, and finally to him. "We're not, are we? I mean, in some faraway country."

"I told you. We're still in Montana, not far from where we met."

"But that's not possible, Rosh. There was at least two feet of snow on the ground. And here? This is like springtime. It doesn't make sense."

"The Hidden has the same weather year round. It never snows or gets too cold or too hot. We have enough rain to keep things green, and there's always plenty of sunshine." Walter shrugged. "How else could we run around without much on our bodies?"

"But how? It's like you're telling me that this place is magical. Like a Shangri-La deep in the middle of the Montana mountains. Did we come through a secret passageway? Because I sure don't remember it if we did."

Renkon decided he had to help explain. "Actually, you're very close to getting it right. The Hidden is magical. Oh, I don't mean as in hocus-pocus kind of magic. But in the fact that it's a place that was meant for supernatural beings like us."

She gaped at him, and it was apparent that she was trying her best to understand and believe him. Would she believe them more if they showed her?

"I did bring you through a secret passageway. Do you remember when we jumped off the cliff and into the waterfall?"

She studied Rosh. "I remember getting thrown off the cliff and into the water. But nothing after that until I woke up inside this hut."

"That scared the hell out of us when Rosh brought you here and we couldn't get you to wake up." Walker touched her leg.

She studied his hand on her leg but didn't take it away. "Go on."

Renkon cleared his throat before he spoke again. The fact that she let Walker rest his hand on her leg was encouraging. Was she starting to accept them? Or was she only ready to let Walker in because she didn't know he was a werewolf, too?

Renkon checked his cousin. Walker's gesture hadn't gotten Rosh upset. Had the two of them really come to an understanding? If so, then getting Shay to accept the three of them had a better chance of succeeding.

"One reason that The Hidden has remained a secret is that you can only come and go during certain times. They're called The Time of Coming and The Time of Leaving. We can sense when it's the right time, and Rosh knew he could bring you through. When you two jumped into the water, he pulled you through the underwater entrance and brought you into The Hidden through the lake."

Alarm filled her face. "Are you saying the only way out is a way under the water? Wait. Does that mean you have to somehow get back up the waterfall to leave? But how?"

He wanted to take the fear away not just now but forever. If he had his way, she'd never worry about another thing for the rest of her life. "No, the exit is in another location in the mountains. But again, leaving is only possible on certain days. It's like a portal that opens between our worlds. Those of us who live in The Hidden can sense when it's about to open and close. That way we can tell how long we have on The Outside."

"Tell her the rest." Walker's eyes darkened.

"What's he talking about?"

"Shay, even if the time was right, you couldn't leave by yourself. You have to have one of us to lead the way and get you through. If you tried, you'd never find the way out."

"So I'm stuck here until you decide to let me go? I thought I wasn't kidnapped, but I'm a prisoner all the same."

"Again, I know that's how it seems, but I had no choice."

She rested back on her hands, her eyes clouded in confusion. "This is all too much, and you haven't even told me about the werewolf thing yet." She laughed, a short, caustic sound. "The werewolf thing. I can't believe I'm saying those words."

Walker took his hand off her but leaned forward, his intensity flowing off of him. "Maybe you should take some time to let what we've told you sink in. We can tell you the rest later."

She shook her head vigorously. "No way. I want to hear it all. Keep going."

Rosh grabbed the bottle containing wine and then four cups. "Let's have a drink. I think we're all going to need it."

Shay took her cup, as did the others, and waited for Rosh to pick up the story. She took a long drink, closed her eyes, then opened them and settled her gaze on him.

"The stories you've heard all your life are real. On The Outside, we're ordinary people with regular lives and jobs. I was an attorney, Renkon did all sorts of jobs, and Walker was a plastic surgeon. We did well and had money, but we weren't happy there. How could we be when we had to hide what we were?"

"Werewolves." Her eyes grew big as she turned to Walker, the question she'd asked before written on her face.

"Yes, I'm a werewolf, too. But not everyone in The Hidden is."

Rosh took a drink. "I'm not sure who found The Hidden first because it was so long ago, before records were kept. Some say it was a Sioux warrior. But from that point on, certain people of the supernatural world have used it as a place where we can come, shift without fear of being seen, and run free and wild. As werewolves, we can hunt the regular animals of the forest and get lost in our other side."

"Kind of like a Club Med for supernaturals, but the vacation never ends." Renkon grinned. A little humor never hurt.

"Renkon's right. If we didn't have this place to release and let our other half out, I think we'd go crazy. Other supernatural beings can live on the outside and be fine, but the ones who make it inside here are different. I don't know why that is, but I know it's true."

"So you're telling me that not only are there people like you here, there are more of them on The Outside"—she added quotes around the words—"living with humans, and no one knows it?"

"That's right." Walker helped himself to more wine.

"Holy shit." She chugged the rest of her drink and let him refill her cup. "Are there communities of supernaturals? Like in Los Angeles and places like that?"

"Exactly. And even in smaller towns across the country and spread out over the world. Most of the werewolves, at least, tend to mate two or more men to one woman, so if you see that kind of arrangement, it could mean that they're werewolves."

Her eyes grew big again. "Oh, my God. One of my best friends, Tatum Griffin, is living with three men in Passion, Colorado. She told me they're special and different, but I thought she meant the normal kind of special and different. Could she be involved with werewolves and not know it?"

Renkon wanted to hold her and comfort her. "First, we consider ourselves normal, too. Some of us, from werewolves to fairies to shape-shifters, were born the way we are. Other shifters were made, changed by someone else. But to answer your question about your friend, no werewolves would do that without the woman knowing what they are. But, yeah, it's possible that she's involved with supernaturals. I've heard that Passion has a fairly large shifter community."

She put her cup down and put her hands over her face. Was she crying? Had they told her too much, too soon?

* * * *

This is crazy. I'm sitting in a hut with three gorgeous men who are telling me they're werewolves. And that they live in a hidden world deep inside a mountain.

She dropped her hands and swallowed hard. She wasn't dreaming, not when Walker's touch was real enough to send shivers through her. Even after all they'd told her, she ached to pull them to her and let them do whatever they wanted to her body.

"Are you okay?"

Renkon, the more easygoing one of the three, stared at her, worry making lines in his forehead where usually there were none. She didn't want to be the cause of that. "Yeah, I'm okay. I just need a little time. But you have more to tell me, don't you?"

"You need to know about Burac and The Cursed." Walker fisted his hands. "After what they almost did to you, I could throttle each and every one of them."

"It's one of the few things we agree on." Rosh shot her a soft look. "Aside from you, of course."

"What are they? Another kind of supernatural?"

"Yes and no." Renkon's tone was mellower and filled with pity. "They're...different. We don't know why it happened since they came into being a long time ago, but the tales say that they were born to werewolf parents but they couldn't change. You see, werewolf babies will transform within a few weeks of being born. It's only a quick change, and I won't lie, it's painful, but it gets their body ready to morph into a full werewolf later on. But the legend says that The Cursed tried to go through the change and made only a partial transformation. They're stuck between their human and werewolf bodies."

"So that's why they look the way they do." As hard as it was to believe that she could feel anything but revulsion toward Burac and his kind, her heart bled for them. "That's the thing that I almost hit before I ran off the road. So they're in the real world, too?"

"Only Burac can leave The Hidden. The others don't have enough power. But he can't go far."

"Thank goodness. I'd hate to think of those things running around the city."

"If they got out, they'd expose not only themselves but all other supernaturals, too. We're trying to make sure that Burac can't leave, but sometimes he manages to get out for a short time."

"Our ancestors lived in a different era, when only the strong could survive. Nonetheless, they couldn't bring themselves to kill the poor things so, once the babies had grown into children, they brought them here to live or die on their own."

"But surely their parents loved them. How could they abandon their children?" She didn't care what problems a child of hers might have, she could never turn her back on him.

"It was a harder time. Our kind was barely surviving. They did what they thought was best for the pack."

She understood what Rosh was saying, but it didn't make her feel any better about it. "Obviously some of them survived."

"They did and even flourished, breeding among themselves."

"It's why they hate the rest of us." Renkon took a drink then set his cup down. "Their kind wants revenge for abandoning their ancestors, but I think their hatred is fueled by jealousy, too. They want what we have, our homes and our families. Instead, they live like brutal animals, unable to control their beast sides. They try to harm us whenever they can, but they're cowards at heart. Although they'll attack groups, most of the time, they wait to catch one of us alone."

"Have they killed anyone?" How close had she come to losing her life?

"Not until recent years."

"About thirty years ago, Burac was born. He's more intelligent than the rest, but he's also crueler. He rules over them, and they do as he commands. Until he came along, they'd never managed to kill one of us. He wants to rule The Hidden."

"Tell her what else he wants." Walker rose and paced to the door to pull back the flap. He stood, staring into the night.

Rosh didn't answer right away. Instead, he and Renkon bowed their heads, keeping their gazes from hers.

"Tell me, Rosh." Her words came out a whisper.

Rosh lifted his head, his dark eyes flashing bits of amber. "He wants you."

Chapter Six

She was a strong woman, both in body and in mind, but she couldn't hide the panic Rosh saw in her eyes. If he could take away her fear, he would. But maybe being afraid would make her realize how close she'd come to disaster.

"Why does he want me?"

She had to know, had to be ready if Burac tried anything else. "The Cursed believe that if they mate with a human woman, then their children will have more human blood running in their veins. Then their children's children can mate with a human and dilute The Cursed's bloodline even more. They think that it will eventually bring their race back to human form and might even allow them to leave The Hidden."

"He wants to mate with me?" Her hand came to her throat. "Oh, crap. That totally sucks."

Her spunk always made him smile. "You can say that again. But we won't let him get to you. Or at least, we'll do our best provided you listen to us and stay put."

The flash of anger in her eyes brought him relief. After everything she'd gone through and all that they'd told her, she wasn't ready to acquiesce to his orders. Still, she had to realize that they were only trying to keep her safe. "It's for your own good."

"You can understand that, can't you, Shay?"

Renkon's softer approach reached her, as he saw the fire in her lessen. "Yeah. I can."

"Good. Then we won't have to worry about chasing after you again, right?" He knew he was pushing, but he had to make sure.

"I said so, didn't I?" She tugged her dress over her knees. "I'll stay until you can take me home."

"If you still want to go by then, I will. But I'm hoping you'll want to stay on. In the meantime, promise us that you'll get to know the others. Look at how they live. Look at how they love."

"I think I already got an eyeful of that part of their lives." The corners of her mouth twitched up.

"I'm not talking about sex. I'm talking about how they treat each other. Get to know the people of The Hidden. Get to know us better before you decide. Can you promise that you'll do that?"

"I can live with that. And until I leave, I sleep here? Alone?"

Rosh felt his cock twitch in anticipation. "Yes. But not alone. Renkon and I will be here."

"And me." Walker faced them, his eyebrow lifted to dare Rosh to argue.

Rosh ground out his words. "We haven't told her about that."

She crossed her arms over her chest. "It seems you didn't tell me a lot of things. So spit it out. What else don't I know?"

"We want you as our mate."

She gawked at Renkon. "As your mate? You want me to what? Live here for the rest of my life? With all of you?"

Rosh tossed a hard look at Walker. "When I brought you inside, that was the same as declaring to the others that I intended to take you as a mate. Along with Renkon. We've wanted to find one woman to share since we were teenagers living on The Outside. I thought that all came to an end when Renkon left home and didn't return. But I found him, along with The Hidden, and we're here to stay."

"I want you, too. I knew it from the first second I saw you."

Walker glanced at Rosh as though expecting him to argue, then went on. "In The Hidden, a woman has the right to choose who she will mate with. If one man doesn't like the next man she's chosen, then he can decide whether or not to stay with her. But I've never seen anyone turn down their mate or refuse to accept her choice in a lover."

"Although Walker and I aren't exactly friends, we both care for you and want you as our mate, along with Renkon. I think caring about you has made us see the light. We'd do anything for you. Even if that means accepting each other."

Walker chuckled along with him. "He's not right a lot of the time, but this time he is." He winced at Rosh's glare. "Sorry. That didn't come out right."

"What these two are trying to say is that the three of us have fallen for you. We love you, Shay. Sure, we've only known you for a short time, but as far as we're concerned, love doesn't have a learning curve. We knew you were the one before you'd even opened your eyes. We want you as our mate for the rest of our lives." Renkon touched her hand. "If you'll have us."

"So let me make sure I've got this right. All three of you want to be my mate. Together. At the same time and sleeping in the same bed? Holy shit."

Rosh couldn't tell if that was a good "holy shit" or a bad one. "You don't know us well, I realize that, and we don't know you very well, either. But werewolves have a sixth sense about these things. Most of us recognize the woman we want as our mate within a few days, even a few hours of meeting her. Humans call it falling in love at first sight. It's rare for humans, but for my kind, it's the rule rather than the exception."

"My father fell in love with my mother two hours after they met. He said he knew she was the one when she took a huge bite out of his ice-cream bar then wouldn't give it back." Renkon was all smiles. "Love isn't logical, especially when dealing with werewolves."

"You can say that again. Nothing has seemed very logical from the moment I woke up here." Her mouth parted, tempting him to kiss her, as she gaped at Renkon. "Wait. Does that mean you were born a werewolf?"

"Yeah. All three of us were, but not all werewolves are. Some are born and some are changed." Rosh hoped they weren't overwhelming her with everything they were telling her. "If you agree to stay, you can decide to stay human or you can become a werewolf. But don't think about that part yet. Make that decision later."

"Shay, do this for us. Try listening to your heart before deciding. Humans may not have the instincts we do, but they do have intuition. After a few days, we'll ask again for your decision."

"We'll accept whatever you decide." Walker pivoted to glance outside again then turned back. "We'll leave you alone for tonight so you can think. But soon, we're going to want to lie with you."

Rosh didn't want to leave her tonight or for any night in the future, but he realized Walker's idea was best. He had to give her time. "Renkon and I will sleep outside the hut and take turns standing guard. None of The Cursed has ever ventured this close, but I don't want to take any chances."

"I'll take my turn watching, too," added Walker.

He stood and let Walker then Renkon go outside before facing her. "But if Walker snores too much and keeps you awake, just say so and I'll smother him for you."

"Sure. Will do." She shot him a smirk then gaped at him. "You're not serious, are you?"

He shrugged and ducked out of the hut.

* * * *

Shay stretched the sleep out of her body and looked through the opening in the top of the hut. Judging from the slant of the shadows, it was still early. Even after the harrowing day she'd had and all the revelations the men had told her, she'd slept peacefully, dreaming of the three fascinating men who'd taken her world and turned it upside down.

But what of the things they'd told her? She'd seen them change, but she still had a difficult time believing that werewolves existed.

How could three amazing men change from human to wolf and back again? Had the stories and legends told the truth?

She shivered as she remembered The Cursed. If anything could convince her that supernatural beings existed, it was those poor creatures. Repulsed, she couldn't bear the idea that their leader wanted to make her his by planting his seed in her to give birth to a child. What would such a child be like? Could she love the child even if it was more like its father than her? She pulled the blanket up to her chin. No, she'd rather die before she let Burac or his kind impregnate her.

"Is she awake?" Rosh's voice was still strong even though he whispered.

"I don't know. Want me to check?"

Renkon. She smiled. He had an infectious laugh and a quick grin. He was a nice counterpoint to his cousin's serious and often hard manner.

"Naw. Let her sleep. We threw a lot at her yesterday."

"Yeah. Maybe too much. But what choice did we have after she saw Burac and then us?"

"None. But let's give her some time. Let her get to know everyone."

She turned onto her side and waited in the silence that followed. Had they left?

"Do you think she'll stay, cousin?"

She held her breath. What would Rosh say?

"I don't know, and I don't even want to go there. I can't imagine life without her now. I love everything about her, even her fiery nature. What about you?"

Her breath rushed out of her then quickened. She bit her lower lip, mesmerized.

"Yeah, I feel the same way. She's it for me. She's more than we ever wanted. More than I'd dared hope for."

"Not too bullheaded?" Walker's voice came from the other side of the hut.

I'm bullheaded? Her stubbornness was like a VW Beetle compared to his Mack truck.

Renkon's wonderful laugh took away a bit of her irritation. Would that be what life with them would be like? Rosh being irritatingly sexy with Renkon's humor soothing the conflict between them? And what about Walker and Rosh? Would she have to referee their arguments? Although, they appeared to have settled their differences. All three men made her hot in a good way. A very good way.

Renkon chuckled. "Are you kidding? I love her spirit and fight. How many other women could've handled all this? Hell, most of the women I know on The Outside would've curled into a ball and cried their eyes out."

"That's true. She might annoy the hell out of me, but I still want to throw her around and shove my cock inside her." Rosh groaned, and she imagined him flexing his muscles so that they rippled with power.

Her body heated as the memory of Rosh on top of her came back. Maybe she should invite them into the hut.

"About that. You and Walker have had a go with her. It's my turn next. How else is she going to know if she wants me, too?"

"Yeah, yeah. Your time will come."

"Besides, you two interrupted us." She could sense Walker standing up and stretching.

She was enthralled by what they said. The way they'd spoken of her, their tones wondrous and deeply sensual, touched a place in her heart that no man had ever reached.

"We're very lucky that it happened the way it did, cousin. Who knows how long it would've taken to find a woman like her on our own."

"Our ancestors must be looking out for us."

"Wow. I didn't think you believed in that kind of thing. You sound like Walker."

"Hell and damnation, don't compare me to him."

"Yeah, he pales in comparison, man," joked Walker.

Renkon chuckled. "Come on, guys. Each of us wants her, and she might end up choosing all of us. We're all in love with her already, so cut out the hostility and get along, okay? Besides, I think most of the huffing and puffing between you two is fake. Give the alpha routines a rest and let's work on getting her to stay."

She smiled at Rosh's and Walker's grumbles. Renkon was right. They were both a couple of boys too caught up in a pissing contest to let it go. She hugged her knees to her chest. They cared for her and wanted her to stay. No wonder she couldn't stop smiling. Had she found what her friend Tee had? If so, she'd be a fool to turn them down.

"We'll need to respect what and who she wants. Both of you need to realize that. Come on. Let's do some hunting today and clear our minds. It'll give her more time to think." Walker cleared his throat. "What do you say, Rosh? A truce? Possible co-mates?"

"I say a day in the woods sounds good."

Throwing off the blanket, she tugged on another dress, similar to the first one, that had been left by the bed along with a comb and a soft towel. A bowl of fruit as well as water sat on a wooden tray nearby, and she hurriedly ate a banana then drank a cup of water.

She ran her palms down her dress to smooth it out then pulled open the flap. Unlike her first day in the camp, lots of people were scattered around the area. Groups laughed as they shared food while children ran and played near the edge of the forest. Woman gossiped as they prepared vegetables and men challenged each other in wrestling matches. The whole thing would've looked like a scene from a historical movie about Native Americans except that the people varied from one ethnicity to the other. Modern-days tools were used as men worked on the roof of one of the cabins and a few of the women wore jewelry that she doubted was handmade.

Okay, Shay, time to get to know the natives.

She stepped out of the hut and hadn't taken two steps before a petite woman, the same woman who had berated Rosh, entwined her arm in hers.

"Hi, I'm Myla. It's about time you got up."

Shay flushed with embarrassment. "I'm sorry. I didn't know I was supposed to get up, and I didn't see an alarm clock." They'd left her phone on top of the cliff along with her other clothes.

"Don't worry about it. Once you're here long enough, your internal clock will wake you up on time. Besides, the men wanted you to sleep in."

"Oh, I don't know if I'm going to stay that long." Yet as soon as she'd said the words, her gut tightened. Did she want to leave? Could she return to her old life? A life without the men who loved her?

Myla released her arm and whirled to confront her. Her brilliant emerald eyes flashed with fire, making her red curls seem like a flame. "Are you kidding me? Don't be ridiculous. Why wouldn't you want to stay?"

"Because this isn't my home."

Myla's fuse burned out as quickly as it had come to life. "Don't worry, it will. Especially since you have the best-looking, bravest men chasing after you."

Her description of Rosh, Walker, and Renkon was dead-on. "Maybe so, but that doesn't mean I'm ready to pack it in and live in the woods. No matter how beautiful it is." *Or how sexy they are.*

"Wow. I didn't expect that. If they wanted me, I'd jump at the chance."

"Then why don't you?" *Shut up!* Her jealousy warred with her independent streak.

Myla laughed and took her hand. "Because I know they've set their sights elsewhere. Besides, I've already found my true loves. I shouldn't ask for more than my fair share."

"Your true loves? Do you really believe in true love? In soul mates?"

She looked taken aback. "Of course I do." She tilted her head, searching Shay's face. "Love doesn't have anything to do with knowing what another person likes or dislikes. Real affection isn't a result of a list of characteristics fed into a computer. True love comes from your heart and your soul, not from your head. Everyone on The Outside has forgotten how to recognize real love when they see it. They're too busy with work, money, and running as fast as they can until they can't run any longer. Don't you believe in true love?"

Until she'd met the men, she would've answered quickly with a resounding no. "I'm not sure anymore."

Myla nodded sagely. "You will. Give your heart time to relearn how to know your true loves when you find them. When it does, you won't have any doubts."

Shay let out her frustration in a quick puff of air. "So you're with other men?"

"For a time I was mated to four great guys."

"Was?" She caught the sadness in the woman's eyes. "Damn. I'm sorry. I didn't mean to pry."

"It's okay." Myla held her head high. "I had five blessed years with my men before they were attacked and killed by The Cursed."

Shay stopped in her tracks. "Those things killed them?"

"They did."

"Oh, my God. Was there a war?" Yet it was difficult to imagine the peaceful people around her charging into battle.

"Some of the men wanted to exact revenge, but I begged them not to."

"Really?" She blushed at her bluntness. If The Cursed hurt Rosh, Renkon, or Walker, wouldn't she want them punished? "I'm sorry, but why wouldn't you want them to pay for murdering your mates?"

Myla touched her hand and squeezed. "Hate only breeds hate, and bringing more hate into The Hidden would only tarnish the magic here. Besides, I couldn't bear the thought of anyone else getting hurt. Would killing them have brought my men back? Then what good would it have served? I forgave The Cursed and, since it was my decision, The Council respected my wishes."

"You're a better woman than I, Myla. I don't think I could've done the same."

"It was purely selfish on my part. I forgave them so my daughter and I wouldn't let the anger fester inside us. I did it for us, not for them."

"Your daughter?"

She laughed and gestured toward a young girl with red hair as she dashed by them. "Yes. My mates gave me my wonderful daughter, Kira."

Kira squealed as a lanky boy grabbed for her. She dodged him and ran toward one of the cabins, tossing off her clothes as she did. Turning around to make sure he was still in pursuit, she giggled then waved at her mother. Within the next minute, Kira was gone and a snow-white bunny replaced her.

"Holy shit. Did you see that?"

"See what?"

The bunny hopped away, and the boy tried to catch it. "Your daughter. She changed into a rabbit."

Myla tugged on her arm, turning her in the opposite direction. "That's my baby. She loves changing into bunnies and fawns the most. In fact, she was the fawn you saw that day on the road."

"I can't believe this." She yanked on Myla. "They told me they were werewolves, and I saw them change. But when they said there were other supernatural beings here, I guess I couldn't wrap my head around it."

Myla patted her hand like an old woman would do when handing out sage advice. But Shay would've guessed her to be about her own twenty-five years. "You'll get used to seeing things like that. But other wonders abound here, too. All you have to do is accept what your eyes are telling you."

She glanced around, studying the people harder than before. "Can everyone here change?"

"No, only the shape-shifters and the weres. You know, like your men. Werewolves. Although we do have werecats, werebears, a couple of werecoyotes, and a few weredeer. We even have a werebadger, but he keeps to himself, the grumpy old fart."

"I thought werewolves and shape-shifters were the same thing." She turned loose of Myla's hand as a butterfly glittering with tiny diamonds on its wings flew by. "Oh, how beautiful!"

"Werewolves are a kind of shape-shifter, but a true shifter like my daughter and me can change into any animal."

Flowers in colors Shay had never imagined lined the area behind one tent. "What about people? Can shifters change into other people?"

"Shape-shifters have the ability to transform into people, but we have a rule against that. If we didn't, all kinds of chaos would break out."

She stopped as an idea struck her. "What about the children and the nudity? I mean, don't you worry about what they'll see?" Her gaze dropped to her crotch then lifted back to Myla with arched eyebrows. "You know. Men's dingalings and women's yoo-hoos?"

"Dingalings and yoo-hoos?" Myla clamped a hand over her mouth to stifle her giggle. "What silly names. You mean penises and vaginas?"

"Sorry. A friend of mine calls them that." She had to tell Tatum to stop using euphemisms so they wouldn't rub off on her.

"Being naked is the natural way for us. Our children learn from the very beginning that everyone's human body is as beautiful as their animal form. I don't think they even notice any longer."

"But you sent them inside a cabin when everyone got involved in the orgy."

"I don't mean this in a critical way, but you really have a lot to learn. That wasn't an orgy. To us, an orgy is for sexual pleasure and doesn't always involve love or caring. What you saw was spontaneous lovemaking. Everyone was with their mates and expressing their love for one another. But we don't allow the children to see or hear us. They must grow up and learn the other ways to show love such as helping one another and treating everyone with respect and kindness. Once they're adults and have found their special ones, only then can they join in and express their love in a sexual way."

"That's good. So let me get this straight. Nudity is okay, but no sex in front of the kids."

"That's about it."

"Then why do any of you wear clothes at all?"

Myla blinked at her then touched her on the arm. "We don't. Not usually. But we knew you'd feel more comfortable if we did. Just as when we disappeared the day you came awake. We didn't want to overwhelm you."

Myla bent to brush her palm over the tops of the flowers. The flowers moved, not merely swaying from her touch but bobbing up and down as though they were dancing.

The buck that had blocked her way out of the hut the first day bent over to allow a small boy to climb onto his back. The boy whooped and hollered, hanging on to the buck's antlers as the buck lifted his front legs into the air.

"Is he one? The buck? He wouldn't let me leave the hut."

Myla giggled, sounding much like her daughter. "I heard about that. They didn't want you to run off and get hurt, so they chose Nicolas to stand guard. They figured a buck wouldn't frighten you as much as a bear or wolf would."

"They were right about that."

Myla waved to a group of women. "I'll leave you to look around on your own. But please, because of The Cursed, don't wander off."

"I won't." She'd promised she wouldn't, and besides, she was too curious to leave. How had she fallen into a fairy tale filled with mystical creatures and amazing people? Not to mention three men who wanted her. She turned in a slow circle, taking in everything.

What would it be like to live here? Right now, it all seemed wonderful and new, but would the beauty and allure of The Hidden fade?

And what about Renkon, Walker, and Rosh? She'd never felt as close to any man as she did with each of them. Especially not in such a short time. Her gaze drifted to Myla, who helped braid a child's hair. Was true love real? If she let herself believe, would she realize that she'd fallen in love at first sight with three men?

Suddenly, she wished she could call Tatum. Although many of her friends had enjoyed ménages, none of them lived with more than one man. Except Tee. "If only I had my cell phone."

"It wouldn't do you any good."

She spun around and found an old man standing behind her. His face was weathered and wrinkled and covered with his long white beard, and his blue eyes held a kindness that made her trust him. "I'm sorry?"

He held on to the top of a cane that showed many rings to denote the age of the tree it had been carved from. "My name is Charlton, Shay."

"How do you know my name?"

The laugh lines around his eyes deepened with his smile. "We all know your name. It is you who have not learned ours."

She didn't take offense at the gentle rebuke. "I'm learning a few today. Don't you have any cell phone reception here?"

"No. We don't have electricity here, either. Or cell phone towers, television, tablets, or even e-book readers."

"I guess I should've guessed judging from your homes." At his lifted eyebrow, she hurried on, careful not to offend him. "I mean, they're nice and all, but this girl likes her cable television."

He pressed the tip of his cane to the bottom of her chin. "Young one, the comforts of The Outside are nothing compared to the treasures The Hidden gives us. You'll learn that and many other things in time."

"But why not have the modern comforts and the treasures, too?"

He leaned on his cane again. "Once you have the fruits of this world, those other comforts become meaningless." He winked, patted her on the shoulder, and shuffled past her.

She watched his slow progress across the camp, noting how the others bowed with respect whenever he drew close. *I feel like I just met Obi-Wan Kenobi. Who's next? Yoda?*

"Take him inside the cabin!"

A nude Rosh and Walker burst out of the trees. They carried Renkon, his head hanging low, his feet dragging on the ground, and a long line of red tracking over his broad chest.

Chapter Seven

Shay's breath caught in her throat, and her first instinct was to reach into a nonexistent pocket of her dress. "This is why you need cell phone service," she grumbled.

Taking off at a run, she followed the crowd of people helping the men carry Renkon up the slope and into the first cabin. Everyone milled around them as they strode through the open living room and through the adjoining huge kitchen. Rosh pushed his shoulder against a door, banging it open before hauling Renkon inside.

The interior of the cabin was rustic with wood-carved furniture. Candles and lanterns rested on rough ledges and mantels. Large beams crossed the expanse of the ceiling while blankets not unlike the ones she slept with covered the walls. Shutters lay against the walls next to the windows, ready to block the view at night.

Shay made it to the bedroom door, but too many people prevented her from entering. Peeking around the others, she watched as Rosh and Walker gently laid Renkon on top of a four-poster bed. Blood seeped from a long wound running from his neck to below his rib cage. His face was pale and his eyes were closed.

"Is he dead?"

Anger flashed through her at the unknown speaker. She couldn't fathom why anyone would tempt fate by asking the question.

He can't be dead. Not now. I can't lose him.

"No. He's alive," answered Walker.

Her knees almost buckled with the flush of relief. *Thank God. I don't think I could stand it if he died.*

"What happened?" Charlton eased past her, and the crowd parted for him like subjects making way for their king.

"Burac and a couple of his pack jumped him as he changed into his human body. He didn't have a chance to defend himself." Rosh stepped back, allowing Charlton to bend over Renkon.

"It was a premeditated attack." Walker's expression hardened as those around her gasped. "They must've tracked us and waited until we split apart. We were trying to flank a deer when it happened."

"Planned? Since when do The Cursed plan attacks?"

Charlton's blue eyes latched on to her. "Since Burac is desperate to get what he wants."

A chill swept over her as those around her turned to look at her. "This is my fault? But why attack Renkon? Why not try and abduct me instead?"

"There's no way to know for sure, but I believe he's sending us a message." Charlton's tone was harsh, but controlled.

"Charlton's right." Walker pivoted to face the crowed. "He's sending us a warning. We know what he wants. Either we give it to him or else."

He wants me. "Or else what?" She wasn't sure they'd heard her whisper until Rosh answered.

"Or else it's war."

She glanced at Myla, who stood near her. "No. I don't want anyone else hurt because of me. I-I'll give him what he wants. I'll go to him."

Rosh and Walker both shook their heads, their eyes blazing with amber, fangs slipping from between their lips. Rosh strode to her and took her arm. "Don't even think about it. We won't let you."

"He's right." Walker scanned the crowd. "We've let them get away with far too much already, but no longer. It's time we fight back."

Everyone started talking at once. Shay stood, her arm still held by Rosh, as emotions whirled inside her. She'd give her life for not only her men, but for the people of The Hidden.

"No."

He hadn't raised his voice, but Charlton's words brought silence. "We don't do anything. The Council will meet and come to a decision. Until then, stay in the campground and keep your children close to you."

She opened her mouth to resist, to demand he let her make the sacrifice, but he held up his hand to stop her.

"You will stay with one of your men at all times. If not, we'll have to find another way to keep you here."

Rosh's tightening of his hold warned her to stay quiet. She gritted her teeth against the rebuke on the tip of her tongue.

Charlton waved his hand over Renkon's forehead. "He has a fever. Look at this wound. Burac must've cut him with a knife tainted with poison. That can only be Burac's doing. The rest of The Cursed don't have the intelligence to handle poison." The old man grimaced as he straightened up. "Where is Penn?"

People turned to look back out of the bedroom. Shay did the same even though she wasn't sure who Penn was.

A woman dashed toward them carrying a large wicker basket. She had long white hair that was twisted into one braid that bounced as she ran. She moved away from the door as the others did, giving the short, broad woman room to enter.

"I'm here, Charlton. I gathered my herbs first. Lena, bring me cool water and some cloths."

A young girl at the edge of the group spun around and headed toward the adjoining bathroom.

"Are you kidding me?"

The others pivoted to stare at her.

"What do you mean, Shay?" Yet she had the impression that Charlton knew exactly what she was thinking.

"We need to get him to a hospital. This isn't the time for herbs and voodoo."

She'd have felt better if they'd laughed at her. Instead, they responded with grumbles and more than a few snarls. Lena returned with a pitcher of water and white cloths. She put them on the side table and backed away, leaving Penn to take charge again.

"Penn has the power to heal." Walker held out his hand for her to bring her closer to Renkon. "It's not voodoo, and it's much better than any doctor or hospital. Trust me on that."

The closer she got to Renkon, the worse she felt. A knot twisted in her stomach and a stabbing pain splintered into her chest. She slid her hand out of Walker's and took Renkon's as she settled onto the side of the bed.

Tears sprang to her eyes, blurring everything, and she held on tight, praying her touch would make him open his eyes.

Penn took the other side of him, bent over, and placed her hand on top of his wound. He moaned then settled as she drew her hand to her nose and sniffed. "It's poison, all right, and it's moving through his blood toward his heart."

Shay wiped away a tear and forced herself to not let another one fall. "Can you help him?"

Penn's bright hazel eyes pierced into her. "I can. But your love can do more than any medicine I have. Perhaps together, along with his werewolf blood, we can. Let's hope it's enough." She stood and flung her braid back behind her. "Everyone, get out of here."

"I'm not going anywhere." Shay jutted out her chin, but she needn't have worried.

"I wouldn't expect you to." Penn flicked her hand at Rosh, Walker, and Charlton. "You men get out. This is for Shay and me alone."

She focused on Renkon, only vaguely aware of the others moving out of the room and someone closing the door. Penn pulled out several plants, none of which she recognized, and started mixing them together in a bowl. Who knew what kind of magic the woman could work? She didn't care as long as it made Renkon better.

Closing her eyes, she put Renkon's hand between her two and

said a prayer, easing the horrible feeling of helplessness churning inside her. If she could think of anything else to do, she'd do it. If Penn told her to jump off another cliff, she'd happily run to the edge and fling herself off.

How had she come to care for him so much? She'd barely spoken to him, and yet she sensed that she knew him as well as those few close friends she'd had her entire life. And she didn't feel that way just for Renkon. As though the attack had opened a gate inside her, feelings flowed outward. Walker, Renkon, and Rosh were as much a part of her as the breath she drew. Myla had spoken the truth. Love had nothing to do with knowing what foods a person liked or if they had siblings or a great job. Love came from a sense of connection, a primal instinct that foreshadowed the ability to learn and grow together. Those in The Outside had corrupted what true love meant and could no longer recognize it without needless trappings like romance and sex.

It didn't matter that she didn't know much about them. Their hearts had somehow recognized each other amid all the stubbornness and struggle. She opened her eyes, ready to believe in the unbelievable.

Renkon's blue eyes were the best thing she'd ever seen. "Hey." She glanced up at Penn, who had her eyes closed and continued to chant words in a language she didn't recognize.

He tried to speak, but no sound came out. She shushed him and caressed his cheek. "Don't talk. Just rest. I want you back on your feet as soon as possible."

Even as ill as he was, he managed a grin, but it faded all too fast. He slicked his tongue over his lips and, this time, managed to speak. "What for?"

She pressed her lips to his and hated that he felt so warm. "So I can get you back off your feet as soon as possible."

He rewarded her with another grin then closed his eyes. Alarm stiffened her neck.

"Let him rest. You can stay with him, but don't let him talk." Penn added water to the crushed ingredients in the bowl and stirred it until it became a thick soup. "Now lift his head."

Shay cupped the back of Renkon's head while Penn poured the foul-smelling substance into his mouth. Renkon groaned but swallowed. She repeated the process until all the soup was gone.

"I don't understand. He reminds me of my friend Willa and her husband. That's why I came to the mountain. They were very ill, but it seemed like something else had happened to them. No one, not even the doctors, knew what was wrong."

"Did they have scratches or bites on their bodies?"

"Yes. Both."

"And they were in a stupor or hallucinating, yes?"

"Yes. So you think The Cursed attacked them, too?"

"Yes, it sounds like it. But only Burac can go to The Outside. Your friends were lucky he didn't kill them." Penn passed her palm over Renkon's midsection then made circles over his crotch.

"He's killed humans before?"

"Not yet, but he's getting more and more violent. He's different than the rest of The Cursed. He's truly evil, not simply a brutal animal. He's smart and cruel. He ventures outside in hopes of bringing back a human female, but he's never been able to bring one through. It angers him that he can't. I think he's started attacking humans just for the sake of wanting to inflict pain on anyone he can."

"Then how did Rosh bring me through?"

She shrugged as if they were talking about inconsequential things. "We can bring humans though, but The Cursed can't. I don't know why. Perhaps it's the Universe's way of keeping your world safe."

"But my friends didn't say anything about a creature attacking them."

"Humans don't remember the attacks. The Cursed's venom seeps into their minds and makes them forget."

"But they lived, so Renkon will live, too, right? They were sick a lot longer before they got medical help." Could she call what Penn did medicine? But if it helped, who cared what it was called?

"The Cursed's venom that seeps from the end of their claws can cause hallucinations and erratic behavior along with extreme flu-like conditions in humans, but it's not life threatening. Some humans are even immune. But with Renkon, Burac used more than just venom because he knows a werewolf's blood will counteract the venom. He used another poison on his knife that he knows is deadly to supernaturals."

"Is he going to be all right?" She inhaled as a shudder racked his body. "You're not saying he's going to die, are you? Please don't." She'd give anything to keep him alive. But what could she do? She was helpless, lost in a world she didn't understand.

Penn shook her head. "That's for him to decide and for you to help him."

"What do you mean? How can he decide anything in his condition?"

Penn mumbled a few words then passed her hand over his forehead again. "The poison takes away a werewolf's will to survive. He has to want to live. He has to know that he has a future worth fighting for. You can give him that reason to live."

"Me? But how? Tell me what to do and I'll do it."

"Reach him with your soul. Talk to him, touch him, be with him. If you two were truly meant to be together, he'll hear you and come back to you. You've already roused him once. That's a good sign."

Shay nodded although she wasn't sure how to do what Penn was saying. "He has to live."

"You must know one more thing."

She would've sworn that her heart skipped a beat. "Yes?"

"You know what he is."

"Yes."

"As a werewolf, he may change while the poison is still in his body. His inner wolf will fight to stay alive even if his human half may choose to leave this world. He may shift completely. If he does, I can't promise that he will know you."

She swallowed and fought her own struggle against fear. "But I thought they could. That their human side remained. But you're saying he could hurt me."

"He may not change at all or just part of the way. There's no way for us to know what will happen. But the poison can make him forget who you are. Who everyone is. If he runs into the forest, he may never return, and he'll die alone."

The thought of Renkon alone and suffering chilled her to the bone. But what could she do to keep him here if he turned? She was no match for a werewolf.

"You have to be careful." Penn grew thoughtful. "I should send for Rosh and Walker."

"No." She couldn't believe that Renkon could ever harm her. "I'll be okay."

Penn gathered her materials and put them back into the basket. "If that's your decision, then I've done all that I can. Now it's up to both of you." She crossed to the other side and patted Shay on the arm before hefting her basket in front of her and exiting.

Shay sat with him, unable to think of anything else to do. Could he hear her?

She poured some cold water on a rag and placed it on his feverish forehead. "Renkon, if you can hear me, listen really hard, okay? I'm not into a lot of mushy stuff, so I'm going to say this straight out. I care about you."

She coughed out a sound that was a cross between a laugh and a sob. "I don't know when or how it happened, but you've come to mean a great deal to me. I want you to hold me, to kiss me, to tell me that you care for me, too."

His pale skin frightened her. How could a man so robust, tanned, and filled with life look so dead? She wiped the awful word away. He wasn't dead, and he wasn't going to die. Not if she had anything to say about it.

She choked back another sob. She wouldn't cry. To cry might let him think she thought his condition was hopeless. No way would she let him down.

"Fine. Maybe I am getting a little mushy. So sue me. No, wait. Rosh might actually do that." She smiled and imagined that she saw the corners of his mouth tweak upward. But it was only her imagination.

"Maybe it's this place, or the people, or you three men, but I'm different here. I've always kept going, trying new things, daring to take life for everything it's worth. I think part of me was afraid of slowing down. It's like if I stop moving, I'll find out that I really don't have anywhere to call home."

She took his hand and played with his fingers, moving them up and down so she could pretend that he was the one really in control of them. "Oh, sure, Passion is a great little town with lots of different people and things to do. And it was a great town to grow up in. But I think I left, trying to find somewhere else to live, because I've always felt like a piece of my life was missing. Like I had to find…more. Does that make sense?"

Please wake up. Please. I need you.

"I think maybe I was hunting for you. And Rosh and Walker, too. I know it sounds stupid, like one of those ridiculous romantic comedies, but I can't help it. The longer I stay here, the better I feel. The more I feel for you and for them. You and the other men fill a need that I didn't even know I had. I think I may have finally found my real home."

She laid her head on his chest and closed her eyes. The *thump* of his heart reassured her even though it was neither strong nor regular, but at least it still beat. She yearned to have his arms around her. If he'd heard her and could answer, what would he say?

"Renkon, come back to me. I don't think I could stand losing you."

She felt the growl rumble through his chest a second before she heard it with her ears. Fear formed a roadblock in her throat and made breathing difficult. Slowly, she lifted her head as the fur spread over his body.

Holy shit, he's shifting.

She pushed away from him, never taking her eyes off him as her feet found the floor. His body blurred, but she could still make out his arms and legs bending, breaking with terrible popping sounds. His face elongated and pointed ears replaced his human ones. Claws broke through the ends of his fingers.

She backed up as one of the men she loved changed into a large black wolf. "Renkon, it's me, Shay."

Cold eyes latched on to her as he pulled his lips into a snarl. Vicious fangs dripped with saliva as he came to a crouch on top of the bed. If he leapt at her, he could tear out her throat with one quick slash of his deadly claws. Her back struck the wall, and she glanced toward the door Penn had closed behind her.

If I ran, could I make it out the door before he caught me?

She doubted it. He had to be faster than she, especially when her legs had suddenly locked. Even bending her knees seemed impossible.

"If he runs out into the forest, he may never return, and he will die alone."

Penn's ominous warning made her decision easier. She had to keep him in the room. Even if it meant sacrificing her life.

"Renkon, listen to my voice. You know me. I'm the woman you love."

He growled then jumped off the bed. She cried out, closing her eyes as her legs gave out and she sank to the floor. When she opened them, he was only a couple of feet away from her.

"Please hear me. You know who I am. I won't hurt you."

She almost laughed. *Yeah, like I could totally whoop his furry ass.*

Amber eyes gleamed, but for a moment, she thought she saw

something other than rage in them. "That's right. You know me, Renkon. I'm Shay. If you can't remember me, then try to trust me."

Taking a deep breath along with sending a prayer skyward, she reached out her hand. He tilted his head at her.

He probably thinks I'm some crazy human bitch. She dragged in another breath. *I think he may be right.*

The snarl went away with his whine. He plopped down on the floor, like a pet dog at its master's feet, then started shifting again. Closer than before, she could see his fur disappear as human skin stretched over changing limbs. The long muzzle left, replaced by his nose and chin. Soon, Renkon the man lay at her feet.

She grabbed him, surprised and relieved that his eyes were open. "Renkon, help me get you back into bed. I can't lift you by myself."

He moaned as she took him under his arms and tugged on him. "Come on, man. Do your part. You owe me for scaring the shit out of me."

Whether he heard her or not, or whether he ran on instinct, he struggled to his feet and put his weight on her. Puffing, she managed to get him to the bed and let him fall back. She lifted his legs and straightened his body into a more comfortable position.

"Renkon? No. Don't you dare close your eyes again. You open them this instant."

But his eyes remained closed. "Damn it. You'd better come back to me. I don't play nursemaid for just anyone, you know."

"If anyone can make him come back, it's you."

She bolted upward to find Walker and Rosh standing at the doorway. They made no attempt to draw closer.

Oh, sure. Now they show up.

"We didn't mean to eavesdrop."

"Yes, we did. We could've gone when we first heard you. But we didn't want to."

Rosh shot Walker a quick snarl. "Fine, we heard. But what matters is what you said." His gaze drifted to Renkon. "He loves you as much as we do. Don't try and understand why or how. Don't try to convince yourself that it's not real because it came so fast. What's between us"—he paused, his gaze darting to Walker then back—"all three of us, isn't anything we could have planned."

"We have a saying here." Walker's dark eyes glistened, and she had to wonder if tears were the cause of it. "'When fate gives you a gift, accept it with open arms.' Accept the gift, Shay."

Rosh nudged him. "Let's leave them alone. Renkon doesn't need us. He needs her."

Walker hesitated only for a moment before following his friend back into the living room. She heard the door close after she'd turned back to Renkon.

"It seems you're my gift. Well, then, I accept. But I don't like people who give me a present then turn around and take it away. So listen up, man. You've got to fight that poison. If you don't and you die, then I'm never going to forgive you. You got that? Die and there'll be hell to pay."

Come on. Open your eyes and give me one of your great grins.

He remained still, only the lift and fall of his chest telling her that he still lived. Wanting to feel as close to him as possible, she stood and pulled her dress over her head. Climbing onto the bed, she stretched out next to him and molded her nude body to his. He was hot, too hot, and his sweat dampened her skin. Maybe she could absorb some of the poison, drawing it out of him and into her, where it couldn't kill. She realized it was a fanciful thought, but she clung to the notion even as she closed her eyes and concentrated on sending healing thoughts to him.

Hear me, Renkon. Feel me. I'm here for as long as you want me.

She clung to him, listening to the erratic rhythm of his heart, and willed it to keep pumping. If she could, she'd take his place in the bed. She fell asleep with one thought echoing in her mind.

Stay with me.

Chapter Eight

Renkon awoke to find Shay's arm thrown over his chest. Her naked body was snuggled next to his, and she cradled her head on top of his arm. Her long lashes rested against her smooth skin and dark hair spread over his arm, its silkiness as tempting to touch as her full lips. She was more beautiful than he'd ever seen her.

Had he really heard her speaking to him? Had his pain made him imagine the loving words she'd said? Her words had given him the strength to fight the cruel agony raging within his body. Did he recall the stroke of her hand on his cheek? Or was it only his fever that made him dream that his wishes had come true?

He frowned as another memory pushed the pleasant ones aside. A knife of remorse, more brutal than the blade Burac had used, stabbed into him as he recalled her face stricken with panic, her eyes wide, and her back against the wall. Werewolf amber had colored the sight of her, wiping away his desperate grasp on reason.

And then she'd spoken to him. He struck down the beast inside him, forcing it back under his control. If he hadn't heard her voice, he doubted either one of them would have survived.

But we did, and she's safe in my arms.

He brushed the hair away from her face, and she stirred, moaning in her sleep. Her breasts pushed against his side, already calling his cock to life. He shifted so that he faced her and touched the tip of his finger to her nipple. She arched, reacting to him. Smiling, he rubbed his thumb over the hardening bud then pressed his lips to hers in a gentle caress.

When she rolled onto her back, he paused to study her face. Was she really asleep, or was she faking it? Was she playing with him? Teasing him now that he had recovered? He didn't care. Either way was good.

Easing her head off his arm, he propped himself up then skimmed his fingertip around her areola, down the hollow between her breasts, and to her belly button. She squirmed but didn't open her eyes.

Taking that as a good sign, he continued his descent until he reached the curly mass of dark hair. He twirled a few hairs around his finger then cupped her mons. Taking another look to see if she still had her eyes closed, he flicked his tongue over her nipple and moved his finger between her pussy folds. Her chest rose with a quick inhale of air, but her eyes remained closed.

She was hot, as though she'd been waiting for his touch. He circled her clit, rubbing, but not too hard, not enough to wake her. Yet he knew he should. What would she say if she woke to find his fingers massaging her? Would she take offense, or would she open her legs wide, loving that he'd chosen this way to awaken her?

He took her nipple into his mouth and used his tongue to copy the circles he made below. He dragged in her scent, recognizing it as the same fragrance that had come into his dreams as he lay fighting the poison. He had sensed her just as he could drink in her aroma and feed from her strength now.

Visions of the attack, of Burac jumping out at him in his most vulnerable moment of transition barreled into him. Angry at the intrusion, he gritted his teeth, determined not to let that torturous moment ruin his time with her.

Instead he held on to the joy that had filled him when he'd awakened to find her leg and arm thrown over him, possessing him. She was the one who'd helped him stay inside his body even as his inner wolf cried out in pain. She was the one who'd healed him as surely as if she'd given him a miracle drug.

He slipped lower, deciding that he'd awaken her with an orgasm. Surely she couldn't get angry at him for that?

Easing himself between her legs, he took a moment to drink in the sweet sight of her pussy. He yearned to see her pink bundle of nerves, to press his face to her and draw in her special smell. Closing his eyes, he did just that.

But her fragrance alone was not enough. He pushed aside her tiny folds covering her clit then flattened his tongue against her. She jolted, and he paused, waiting for her to tell him to stop. His cock pulsed in anticipation, but again his doubt took over. He'd never do anything against her will, and until they had lain with each other, he didn't want to assume more.

But was she really asleep? He had to know for certain.

"Open your eyes, Shay. I want you to know who makes you feel this way."

Her giggle was his answer. "Who goes down there?"

"You sneak!" He threw his body on top of hers, holding himself up so he wouldn't crush her.

She giggled again, louder and longer, and slapped a hand over her mouth. He took her hand away to see her grin.

"Holy shit, Renkon. You really didn't think I could sleep with you touching me like that, did you?"

"I had a feeling you were faking it."

"Oh yeah? Then why didn't you keep going if you were so sure?" Her eyes twinkled with mirth.

"Because I prefer a partner who contributes to the lovemaking." He narrowed his eyes. "Or is pretending to sleep not the only thing you fake during sex?"

"Why, you lousy son of a bitch!"

She pushed against him, throwing him to the side, then flung her body over his. Her eyes widened and she tried to climb off of him, but he wouldn't let her go.

"What's the matter?" He was surprised he could speak with her heat pushing against his hard cock. If he didn't get inside her soon, he might have an accident that Rosh and Walker would never let him live down.

"I don't want to hurt you. Damn, how can I have been so stupid? You need more time to recover."

"No, I don't. I'm fine." He dropped his gaze to his chest where the long gash had been. "See? All better."

She skimmed her hand along the already-fading pink scar. "But how? That wound was deep. And the poison?" She shook her head, confusion putting lines in her forehead.

"Penn's potion helped with the poison, and I'll thank her as soon as I can. And it was my werewolf side of me that gave me the strength to hold on."

"And the strength to almost kill me, too."

He saw the regret on her face before she had a chance to apologize. He placed his hand on her throat. If he'd hurt her, killed her, he would've chosen to die soon after her.

"It's okay. I talked you out of it. You were an absolute pussycat in my hands."

"Argh, please don't use 'pussy' and 'cat' in the same sentence."

Her laugh could charm the birds out of the trees. "So you're really fine? No lingering aches or pains?"

"Not a single one. Although I guess I'm still a bit weak."

"Oh, shit. I'm sorry."

She tried to get off him again, but he pulled her back on top. His cock settled into her crotch, pushing at her opening.

"I told you. I'm fine. Don't be sorry. Be wild. Ride me, baby."

"I don't think so."

"What?" Was she playing with him again? He didn't think he could stand another round of pretend.

"I want you to finish what you started. Or shouldn't I say the word 'pussy' again?"

"As long as it's that word by itself, you're good. In fact, you can say that word all the time. Come here." He took her hips and helped her wiggle forward until her crotch was over his face. If Death had come for him at that moment, he would've happily gone.

"Damn, you're beautiful."

"Less talk and more tongue, wolfie."

"Wolfie?"

"Yeah. You got a problem with my calling you that?"

"Does that mean you're not freaked out about what I am? What we are?"

A flash of concern was on her face then gone. If he could've taken the question back, he would have.

"Freaked out? Sure. Especially after what happened while you were ill. But I'm trying not to be. As long as you stay in your human form, I'm good."

"Okay. No changing without warning you."

"Definitely. Keep your skin on."

He pulled her labia apart with his fingers and let his eyes do more feasting. Her clit was swollen and glistening with her heat, ready to explode. Sliding a hand over her rounded stomach, he slid his tongue along her slit in a long, slow stroke. She jerked then let him settle her even closer so that he didn't have to lift his head to drink from her.

He put his mouth to her cunt and pressed his tongue to her hard nub. She moaned, and her juices flowed into his mouth and onto his face. Her sounds of ecstasy grew louder the harder he stroked, licked, and bit her.

Rubbing her stomach, he could see her grasp one breast and torture her nipple. If he had two heads, he would've sucked on her tit as he devoured her pussy. He couldn't wait until he could watch Rosh and Walker as they took her from the front and the back.

She held on to the headboard and tipped her head forward to watch. She couldn't see the smile on his face, but he was sure she could see the happy glint in his eyes. She rocked her bottom, encouraging him to sink his tongue into her pussy. Finding the crease between her ass cheeks, he fingered her dark hole, teasing her from both sides.

Her cry broke free from her as her orgasm ripped away. Warm, sweet nectar flooded into his mouth, and he sucked long and hard, taking in every drop he could get. Tremors racked her as she turned loose the headboard and slid down his chest, drawing a line of her cream along his skin.

She put her forehead to his. Her eyes were clouded with lust.

"We're not finished."

She let out a long breath. "We're not?"

As if she doesn't know.

Instead of telling her, he picked her up and sat her down on his crotch. His cock shoved at her pussy, but he'd hold back until he could see her face as he slid into her. She yelped at his quick move and dug her fingernails into his chest.

"Renkon." She'd spoken his name and followed it with a whimper.

He couldn't hold back any longer. Nothing could stop him now except her flat refusal. But he sensed she couldn't have denied him any more than he could've walked away from her.

Lifting her, he positioned his cock and slid into her pussy. She cried out again as he let out a breath and groaned.

He'd expected her to be tight, but she was so much tighter than he could've imagined. Her pussy walls closed around his cock, and if she hadn't already claimed his heart, she would've done so then. He closed his eyes, letting the sensation of going deep inside her fill his body, his mind, and his spirit.

She pressed her breasts between her arms as she rocked. Her movement was slow at first as though she were relishing the buildup as much as he was. Picking up speed, she started rotating her hips so that she moved in a circle as well as forward and back.

His gaze was glued on her breasts as she shifted again, changing the circular motion into short, quick bounces. Her breasts jiggled enticingly, and he lifted up to catch one between his teeth. Catching her nipple, he bit down with enough pressure to give her delicious pain without causing her harm.

She rode him, bucking with his thrusts even as she ground against him to drive his cock as far as it would go. He plundered her butt cheeks, envisioning his cousin thrusting into her ass as he rammed into her pussy.

Her hair flowed around her shoulders, giving her a dark halo that made her rapturous expression both tender and erotic. Her belly quivered with their lovemaking, and, before he knew it, he was picturing her stomach even larger, filled with a child of their own.

He couldn't hold on much longer. She was too good, too tight, too amazing. Driven to the edge, he held back as long as he could then stiffened with one last attempt to keep from coming.

She tugged on his hair and brought his mouth to hers. Her kiss was rough, her grip on his hair painful, but it didn't matter. Keeping the kiss going, they shouted their releases together.

He fell back onto the pillow and brought her down with him. Enclosing her in his arms, he vowed that he would love her for the rest of his life.

* * * *

Rosh and Walker sat outside the cabin, staring at the front door. They'd never had a close relationship even though they'd gone hunting and on runs together. But since Shay had come into their lives, their attitude toward each other had changed for the better.

He wasn't sure why he'd had a difficult time accepting Walker. Charlton had once said that they were too much alike. The guy was stubborn, cocky, and irritating. But he was also loyal, strong, and ready to help whenever it was needed. All good and bad qualities that he recognized in himself.

Since the day Walker had helped them—helped Shay—at the pond, Rosh had started reconsidering his opinion. He could do worse than Shay choosing him as her third mate.

Rosh could feel Walker's nervous energy. "Are you sensing that? He's awake."

"Yeah."

He let a couple of minutes of silence pass between them. "He's taking her."

"Yeah."

"Without us."

"Yeah."

From his peripheral vision, he saw Walker shoot him a scornful look. "I know."

"Yeah. You should."

He'd taken her, too, but that didn't make him feel any better. Instead of sitting on a large stump next to Walker, he wanted to join Renkon and their future mate.

"No."

Hell and damnation. "No what?"

"No. Let them have this time without us."

"You're mighty generous. Considering."

"Yeah."

Rosh ground his teeth and tried to keep his butt glued to the stump. Other people walked around them, some of them casting them knowing glances and others preferring not to press their luck with Rosh in a bad mood.

"I think we should invite her to the Pledging Ceremony tonight."

Sometimes Walker came up with a good idea. "Okay."

"We might as well get her thinking about it."

"Okay."

"So are we good now? If she wants us both?"

He hesitated, keeping the smugness he felt from showing. *No use in letting him feel too secure.* "Yeah."

Walker shifted in his seat. If he started to head toward the cabin, Rosh intended to stay right by his side.

"Then it's settled."

"The Pledging Ceremony."

"We'll have to clear it with The Council."

He'd forgotten about that, but he doubted they'd refuse. After all, without her Renkon might not have pulled through. "I'll talk to Charlton."

"Good."

Rosh nodded once then stood. Walker hopped up beside him. Without another word, they separated, each going a different way.

* * * *

"Are you sure it's okay for me to be here?" Shay checked the faces of those attending the ceremony. Not a few of them had given her skeptical glances. She wasn't sure why, but it made her uncomfortable.

"I told you it's fine. The Council cleared it. They're a little leery because you're not one of us, but after the way you stuck beside Renkon, they're making an exception." Rosh placed his hand on the small of her back.

"Yet."

She whipped her attention to Walker. "Yet?"

Rosh pulled her close with Renkon coming to her other side and Walker shoulder to shoulder with Rosh. "You know how we feel about you. And we know how you feel about Renkon. You care about me, too, right?"

Walker snarled. "And me?"

Rosh snarled back but didn't take it any further. They'd always share a little push and shove, but they'd have each other's backs, too.

She couldn't deny it. After what had happened to Renkon, she'd realized how much they'd come to mean to her. But did that mean she wanted to pledge her love to them in front of the others?

Not that she could deny the urge to do so. The area they'd chosen for the Pledging Ceremony was under an ancient tree. Its trunk was as wide as an eighteen wheeler and its thick branches spread outward, forming an awning that provided enough cover for all members of The Hidden. Flowers blew in the breeze and soft green grass tickled the bottoms of her feet. As was their custom, they'd come without shoes. Birds provided the music as a young woman and three men stepped forward to stand in front of Charlton. The woman's red hair flowed to the swell of her buttocks with flowers sewn into long braids. The men, all tall and powerful looking, had golden hair that touched the tips of their shoulders. Charlton's long blue robe flowed around him as he pressed his palms together and bowed to the crowd.

"That's Bisna and the Heller brothers."

Rosh's whisper warmed her ear. She wrapped her arm around Renkon. Since Renkon's recovery, she'd felt closer to the men, even having a dream in which they caressed her body and spoke words of endearment to her. Then, in the next dream, they'd taken her like wild men. She loved both dreams.

But one thing had marred her thoughts. They were werewolves. She'd seen Renkon and Rosh in their wolf forms, and although Renkon hadn't harmed her, she still shook whenever she remembered the fierceness in his eyes.

Could she really love three men who might one day turn on her, hurting and perhaps even killing her? Could she leave her life behind and live in The Hidden? They'd told her that they could live on The Outside, but how would that work? Would they end up resenting her for making them leave?

"Bisna, do you pledge to honor the men you've chosen? Will you lie with them at night, keeping their bodies warm and their hearts filled with your love? Will you treasure them as they vow to treasure you? Will you give them a life complete with pleasure and happiness? Will you keep them safe as they will keep you free from harm?"

All eyes shifted from Charlton to Bisna. She tugged on the sleeves of her dress and let it fall to the ground. "I pledge to do these things and more."

Charlton faced the Heller brothers. "Do you, Heath, Harmon, and Hilo, pledge to honor the woman who has chosen you? Will you give her your bodies each night, keeping her warm and her heart filled with your love? Will you treasure her as she vows to treasure you? Will you give her a life complete with pleasure and happiness? Will you keep her safe as she will keep you free from harm?"

Together, the men undid their cream-colored slacks and dropped them to the ground. "I pledge to do these things and more," echoed the three brothers.

Would she ever get used to the nudity in The Hidden? Most of the crowd was naked while a few of them wore clothes, probably in deference to her. Rosh had explained that the people being mated always donned clothes so that they could ceremoniously drop them, revealing their true selves to their mates.

She looked around. At least the children weren't in attendance. Although she understood that they'd grown up unashamed of their bodies and were used to everyone living unencumbered by clothing, she was still uncomfortable with it. Who knew she, Shay Mathews, a free-spirited and fun-loving girl, could be so uptight?

Charlton raised his hands over the foursome. "People of The Hidden, do you accept this union? Do you pledge to honor them as they live and grow together?"

A chorus of "We do" echoed around her.

Rosh, Walker, and Renkon turned to her at the same time and repeated the words. "We do."

Shay ducked her head, unable to respond. She had no doubt that they meant what they'd said. She had, in fact, felt a rush of love from each of them that blanketed her with a sense of belonging, with comfort mixed with an incredible flood of raw, primal desire. Her body trembled at the onslaught of emotions tumbling through her.

They were offering her a lifetime of love and devotion. She'd spent her adult life in casual relationships, never believing that she'd find the kind of relationship she'd only dreamed about. Even more amazing, she couldn't believe that she'd found it with not one but three men.

She was almost afraid to believe her luck, yet at the same time, she wasn't going to miss the chance to grab hold and hang on for dear life.

Rosh gripped her hand and pulled her along with him as everyone walked out of the trees and back to the camp. Women hurried ahead to tend to the food as a group of men rounded up instruments and formed a band. The music lifted to the sky as the sun set behind the trees.

Walker led her to a chair then pulled his chair next to her as did Renkon and Rosh. They sat together in comfortable silence, taking in the festivities. Bisna and her men came into the clearing a short while later, and the crowd clapped and cheered their arrival.

Shay studied the young woman, saw the expression of pure bliss on her face, and knew she wanted to feel that way, too. Standing, she turned to the men and took a deep breath. "I'm going to lie down now. If any of you would like to come along, I'd like that very much."

She turned on her heel, refusing to look back. But she needn't have worried. The sounds of the footsteps followed her.

* * * *

Shay stood on top of the bed of blankets and waited until Rosh, Renkon, and Walker came inside. She needed to tell them what she was feeling, wanted them to know how much they'd come to mean to her, but she couldn't find the words. Instead, she'd show them by having a Pledging Ceremony of her own, one where she'd give her heart as well as her body.

She pushed the bodice of her dress down and shimmied it to the floor. Their hot gazes watched it fall then jerked back up her body, each of them pausing at her dark curls then at her breasts. Her hands covered her breasts, and she tweaked her nipples. Were they already growing hard for her? She licked her lips and found that they were.

Understanding that she wanted to keep silent, they loosened the ties on their pants and pushed them to the floor. Each cock was as huge as the next. Rosh's was curved at the end, promising to hit her sweet spot, while Renkon's was thicker and shorter, like a flesh-and-blood tree trunk. Walker's was longer than the other men's, and the tip of his bulbous cap oozed with pre-cum.

She could already imagine the way their mouths, their tongues, and their hands would feel on her body. Rosh would lick her slit and push his tongue against her clit while Renkon fingered her ass and prepared her for his thrusts. Walker would stroke himself until she demanded that he fuck her mouth.

She lowered herself to the bed and spread her hair in a fan. Reaching out her arms, she offered herself to her men.

Renkon fell to his knees and pushed her legs apart. Walker and Rosh split apart, each coming to her side.

Walker bent over her, cupped her breast, and brought her nipple to his mouth. His tongue whipped around her nipple, and she gripped his arm, squeezing it to let him know how much she enjoyed what he was doing.

She reached out for Rosh and brought him to her other nipple. He bit down, giving her the edge of his teeth. Working his jaws back and forth, he gave her a delightful mix of pain and pleasure. Walker laved her other nipple with attention and took his cock in his hand.

"Stroke your cocks. I want to see the three of you pumping your dicks."

They took their cocks in their hands and started running their hands along their lengths. Walker worked his faster and kept his mouth and his other hand on her breast. Rosh sat back on his heels to work his while he pinched her nipple between his fingers. Renkon played with her curls as he first licked his hand then started masturbating.

They did as she commanded, but she knew they were taking her as though she belonged to them. She inhaled as she realized that she was indeed theirs. But admitting it to herself was different than admitting it to them. No matter how she tried, how close she came to telling them, as when she'd told Renkon that she cared for him, she couldn't force the word *love* out. Showing them was much easier.

She trailed her fingers through Walker's hair and arched her back. Spreading her legs, she silently gave Renkon permission with a lift of her eyebrows to stop pleasing himself and to find out how wet she already was.

He eased her legs farther apart then slid his finger into her seam. "I can smell your juices. You're so wet, so hot."

Rosh picked up speed, pumping his cock harder as he fondled her tit and watched his cousin bring his tongue to her folds. She gripped Walker's hair tighter, needing someone to cling to as Renkon lightly touched her clit. She jerked and widened her legs more.

Walker pulled her nipple into his mouth then let it go with a satisfying pop. She smiled and lifted her arms above her head. She would lie back and let them please her. Wasn't that every woman's fantasy? Not that she would ever deny them their pleasure, but she wanted hers first.

Greedy little bitch, aren't you? Yes. Yes, I am.

Walker moved lower, giving her feathered kisses down her stomach until he found her belly button. She'd never thought of that as an erogenous part of her body, but the way Walker attacked it with his tongue proved her wrong.

Renkon pressed his mouth to her pussy and flattened his tongue against her clit. He slipped two fingers into her pussy, and she clamped around him as surely as if she'd taken his hand and squeezed it with her own. Her pussy fluttered at his touch as he sought out her G-spot.

"Shay."

She turned her head to Rosh and accepted his offer of his cock. Drawing it inside her mouth, she circled the end, drinking off his pre-cum. He fell over her, placing his crotch right above her head and his hands flat on the floor on the other side of her. She skimmed her fingers along his ripped stomach and drew his dick deeper into her mouth.

"Make her come, Renkon. If you can't, then move over and I'll do it for you."

The musky scent of Rosh filled her nostrils as she fondled his balls, earning a groan from him. His balls were heavy against her palm, and she could feel them draw up. He wouldn't last much longer, and she couldn't wait to taste his seed.

Renkon added a third finger to her pussy and increased the pressure on her clit. He grabbed her legs as though he could pull her closer than she already was and drove his fingers into her. His mouth was insistent, demanding that she come.

She mewled, letting the sound flow over Rosh's cock. Walker pushed his cock against her waist and rubbed his pre-cum onto her skin.

"Move, Renkon."

She could feel the sound of Rosh's voice roll through his gut to come out in a guttural tone. His muscles tensed and he thrust his cock toward the back of her throat.

The snarl from Renkon swept alarm through her, and she released Rosh's cock to move her head to the side to look at him. He'd lifted his head to glare at his cousin, his eyes flickering with brilliant amber.

"Keep it together, man. We all want her just as much as you do." Walker gave Renkon the warning, but he sent Rosh a pointed look as well then slid his tongue along her side and over the swell of her breast.

At Walker's warning, the blue retuned to Renkon's eyes and he lowered his head back to her pussy. Latching on to her clit, he pressed his tongue harder than before then curled his finger and found her tender spot inside her pussy. She let out a cry filled with the pain and ecstasy of the orgasm. She bucked uncontrollably as Rosh pushed her onto her side.

She propped her head on her arm and let Renkon lift her left leg over his arm as he got to his knees. His cock rubbed against her still-throbbing clit as Rosh sat up then pushed her far enough onto her side to finger her butt hole. He stretched his body out beside her then caressed her back and nibbled on her neck

"Relax, Shay. We don't need any lube. I'll get you ready and I'll take it easy."

Renkon shoved into her, pushing her body toward the end of the bed. He slammed against her fast and hard, his pelvis thrusting back and forth as he put the pad of his finger hard against her clit. She gasped, stunned at how fast he'd brought her to the brink of another climax, then stiffened and released, screaming out another flush of her cream.

Walker rested back on his legs, then played the tips of his fingers along her lower lip and placed his cock in front of her. She took him in, sucking hard as the shuddering waves tumbled through her body.

"Easy, babe. Breathe." Rosh worked the wet tip of his dick against her butt hole. She didn't have time to tense as he pushed the end into her anus. Easing his length inside her, he spread her wide.

She closed her eyes to enjoy the sensation of three cocks filling her. Renkon's hard shoves seemed like they would meet Rosh's pounding in the middle of her. The tension in her abdomen grew as the heat whirled inside her. She moaned and slid her tongue around Walker's cock, not wanting him to have any less pleasure than the others.

The men spoke words of affection intermixed with dirty talk. Instead of confusing her, she found the combination warmed both her pussy and her heart. Doing both made her feel not only sexy as hell but adored.

Walker's legs strained as he worked his hips back and forth. He tracked his fingers through her hair, supporting her as she fisted her hand around his cock and pulled her mouth along his shaft. His skin slipped between her lips as she skimmed her teeth over it, taking care to not to cross the line between pleasure and pain.

Rosh gripped her hip, keeping her butt cheeks apart. He rammed into her again and again, making her plentiful bottom shake. "I don't think…No. I can't. Aw, hell." He pulled out and spilled his warm seed onto the small of her back.

Renkon groaned then took longer pauses between thrusts. With each shove into her, his expression grew tighter as he strained to keep control. She pushed back, and he dug his fingers into her skin. But the stabs of pain meant nothing to her as she circled her hips and drove him over the edge.

His moan changed into an agonized growl that made its way into a shout. His body jerked as he shot his seed inside her. His cum flowed over her folds and onto her leg.

She pulled Walker's cock out then lay back as Renkon and Rosh moved away. "Walker, fuck me."

He grabbed her, yanking her off the ground and into the air as though she weighed nothing. They fell together with Walker landing on his back. She yelped then laughed as she landed on top of his crotch. Rising, she put his cock at her opening then dropped her body. His dick pierced into her cunt, driving into her like a steel rod.

He took her breasts in his hands and bucked into her, bouncing her as he fucked her. Her hair played along her shoulders as she spread her fingers over his hard chest.

"Damn, but you're tight."

"Too tight?"

"Hell, no."

"Then fuck me harder."

Rosh and Renkon caressed her back, her shoulders, and her hair, but her focus was on Walker. Riding him, she lifted her hair above her head and let Walker fondle her breasts.

They were her men, and she didn't need a real Pledging Ceremony to know that. She had no idea how she could ever bring herself to leave them, and at that moment, she wouldn't have walked away from them for anything in the world.

Walker's eyes flashed amber then went dark again. But she wasn't afraid. None of them would ever hurt her.

With a shove that almost threw her off him, Walker ground out his release. She came a moment later, her release shuddering out her body and into his. Exhausted, she let Rosh and Renkon lift her away and place her on the bed.

They crumpled beside her with Renkon lying between her legs, his head resting on her inner thigh, and the other two men at her sides, as they had been in the beginning. She stretched, luxuriating in the wonderful sensation of having had the best sex of her life. But more, she was certain that the men around her wanted her not for a brief fling but forever.

After a short time, Rosh leaned over her and traced a path along her jaw. "Shay, we want you with us forever. Choose us as your mates. We vow we'll always stay by your side."

Her heart clenched. Why couldn't things remain the way they were? She wanted and trusted them, but love had never been easy for her. Still, she knew they loved her. Of that she had no doubt. But would they always love her? Or would their love fade over time? Was she ready to take that risk?

She took a ragged breath and gave the only answer she could. "No."

Chapter Nine

"No?"

Walker's astonished expression was mirrored by Rosh and Renkon. Had she really turned them down?

He took her by the chin and made her look at him. "What do you mean, no? Don't you understand that we're in love with you? That we'd give our very lives for you?"

"He's right. You're everything to us." Renkon glanced from her to Rosh then to him.

"But why not?" Rosh asked the question that was on his lips.

"I'm not sure what it means to take you as mates. Even the word is strange. Mates instead of partners or husbands?"

"It's only a word. Call us whatever you want." Walker fought against the rising panic. No human who'd come into The Hidden had ever left without pledging herself to the men she'd chosen. What would happen to them if she left them? Would The Council let her leave?

"But you're werewolves." She searched his face for an answer as though hunting for his understanding.

He pulled away from her. "Are you saying you can't handle what we are?"

She shook her head, glancing at each of them. "No, that's not what I mean. I know what you are, and I've come to accept that. I even find it fascinating. But while a human and a werewolf can obviously have sex, can they have everything else? Like a family?"

He relaxed a little. Maybe hope wasn't lost. "We can. You can decide to remain human, or you can become a werewolf. Either way, you can carry our children. If a child is a werewolf, then he or she won't shift until after it's born. If you give birth while still a human, the child will most likely be half-human and half-werewolf."

"Most likely?"

"Nothing is ever totally black and white. Even in The Hidden."

"But know that you'll be the only human in The Hidden. Not that it will matter. Everyone will accept you as most of them already have."

She gave him a rueful smile. "Most of them?"

"A few of the older residents are having a difficult time considering that you were brought here without already agreeing to mate." Rosh shrugged. "But they'll come around."

"I need more time to think."

It hurt more than he thought possible for her not to say yes right away, but Walker had to give her what she needed. Taking his cue from the other men's silence, he relented. "Then take it. Get to know our people more."

"Thank you." She sat up, bringing them along with her. "During that time, I think it would be best if you stayed away from me. At least physically, if you know what I mean."

"But why?"

Walker sympathized with Renkon's anguished question.

"I want to make the decision rationally, and frankly, whenever you guys are around, my thoughts get jumbled up." She smiled and laid her palm against his cheek. "Deal?"

"Reluctantly, yes. Deal."

* * * *

"Should we be out here by ourselves, Myla? You know. Because of…them." Shay hated to sound like a frightened girl, but after the fight with The Cursed by the waterfall and what had happened to Renkon, she didn't want to chance running into Burac and his pack again.

A week had passed since the Pledging Ceremony. In that time, she'd asked the men to leave her alone and they had. At times, she thought it was harder for her than them. Every time she'd see one of them, she ached to rush to him, to tell him to take her and make her his mate. But every time, she'd held back.

What was wrong with her? Why couldn't she tell them how she felt? Why couldn't she accept their love and give them hers? All she had to do was say "yes," but the word stuck in her throat.

Could she live in The Hidden? They'd promised they'd live wherever she wanted, in The Hidden or on The Outside. But it was obvious to her where they wanted to spend their lives. Hadn't they already given up everything to do that? Could she live a primitive life, or would she miss not only the conveniences of the modern world but her family and friends? She'd always lived in the present, never making plans too far ahead, and now three men wanted her to decide the rest of her life.

She rubbed her forehead. Just thinking about it gave her a headache.

"We're okay being here during the daytime, Shay. They don't like coming out in the sunlight. Not that they can't or won't. They simply choose not to."

"Burac attacked Renkon during the day."

"You're right, and we'll be careful. Plus, we're together. I wouldn't go alone, which is why I asked you to come along."

"Oh, so, you're expecting me to keep you safe? Girlfriend, I thought it was the other way round."

She'd meant it as a joke, but Myla's serious expression left no doubt that she hadn't. "Of course I'll keep you safe. We're friends. I know you haven't officially become one of us, but we all know that Renkon, Rosh, and Walker want you to choose them."

Myla grinned, the joy wiping the somberness from her face. "I think if you wanted, they'd have the Pledging Ceremony as soon as they could."

Shay stuck her foot in the chilly water and decided to ignore her new friend's not-so-subtle hint. She wanted to get her mind off the subject for a while. "So are we swimming or what?"

"Of course. But first, I want to show you something."

"What is it?"

Myla wrinkled her nose and shook her head. "Follow me."

Myla led the way over to a large tree then pointed at markings on the lower half of the trunk. Shay bent over and studied them but couldn't make out what they said. The language was strange, hieroglyphic in nature.

"Okay, I give up. What do they mean?"

Myla touched her arm. "They say this. 'To love is to give your mind, body, and spirit. To receive love is to accept responsibility for your lovers' mind, body, and spirit.'"

"O-kay. I get it, but why are you showing me this?"

Myla took her by the arms. "Because, my friend, you are receiving love from Renkon, Rosh, and Walker. It's time you take responsibility for them. Either choose them as your mates, or tell them you want to go home. It'll break their hearts, but at least it's kinder than letting them hope for a future that can't happen."

Shay pulled out of her hold. "Are you asking what my intentions are? Who are you? Their father?" She was only half kidding. Why did Myla think she had any right to force her to make a decision?

"I'm sorry. I didn't mean to upset you. But, as you know, I care about them and I don't want to see them hurt."

Shay stalked away then turned back to confront her. "I don't intend to hurt them. But how can anyone make a decision so quickly? I haven't been here very long."

"And in that time you've watched us, studying our lives and how we interact. I've seen you, and I've seen the longing on your face. You want to join us, I know it. So what's holding you back? Didn't you tell me that you like taking chances, jumping into things without analyzing them to death? Didn't you tell me that you're impulsive and lead with your heart?"

"I did and I am."

"Then why are you hesitating? Is it because of what they are? Because of life in The Hidden?"

"No." Was it true? She'd thought long and hard about their being werewolves and knew she should've run as far and as fast away as she could. "All right. That's partly it."

"You know they'd never harm you. What happened with Renkon was a result of the poison. And still he didn't hurt you." Myla's big eyes held her, pushing her to tell the truth.

"I know." Why wasn't she taking them up on the chance of a lifetime of love? She'd never find any other man who could take even one of their places.

"But you do love them, don't you?"

She answered without giving a moment's hesitation. "Yes."

"Then I don't think it has anything to do with how long you've known them or even what they are."

"Is that so, Dr. Myla? Then tell me. What is your diagnosis of my situation?"

"I think you're afraid of getting tied down."

She opened her mouth to deny it but couldn't. That wasn't true, was it? Granted, she'd always done whatever she wanted, whenever she wanted, and wherever she'd wanted. Aside from growing up in Passion, she'd never stayed in one place for very long. She'd always thought it was because she wanted to see the world, to live life to the fullest, but could the restlessness have come from a different reason? Was she running from getting stuck in one place?

"You have a decision to make, Shay, and you need to make it soon. Either you leave and go on with the life you have, or you commit to the men and reap the rewards of three men who love you with every ounce of their being. Personally, I think it's a no-brainer."

"So I have a deadline? If so, no one told me." She was getting angry, and Myla pushing her into a decision didn't help.

"I'm sure they'd give you all the time in the world. However, The Council is another matter. We've never let any human stay here as long as you have. They've all chosen within days of arriving."

"All of them? So no human has ever come here and decided to leave?"

"I don't think so. No human has ever turned down the men or woman who wanted them as their mate. You'd be the first, if that's what you decide to do." Myla brought her into a quick hug. "Whichever path you choose, know that I'll always be your friend."

Myla tossed her hair back then dropped her dress to the ground. "Okay, let's have some fun."

"Sounds good to me."

Myla giggled, her image blurring. Within a minute, the diminutive woman transformed into a bunny.

"I guess Kira's not the only one who likes hopping around, huh?" She laughed as Myla twitched her nose then scurried around her feet.

"You'd better hope a fox doesn't show up."

The bunny froze then, in the next instant, Myla was standing in front of her again. "Don't ever joke about that."

"Sorry. So is being a bunny your favorite animal to shift into?"

"Actually, no. I like changing into a polar bear." She grinned. "It kind of freaks the werewolves out."

Shay laughed. "I'll bet. I'd like to see that. But I'm ready to go swimming and not with a polar bear. Are you ready?"

"Uh-huh. You'd better hurry and get undressed. Try and catch up with me. If you can." Myla stepped into the water, and her image blurred again until a fish fell from where the woman had been standing and into the water.

"Hey, no fair." She watched as the golden-and-green fish whipped its tail back and forth and disappeared into deeper water. "How am I supposed to keep up?"

She pulled her dress over her head and let it fall on top of Myla's.

"Okay, here I come."

Her breath caught in her throat as a hand covered her mouth. Long nails scraped her cheek, flaring pain that seared inward, traveling down her body. Someone grabbed her around her waist and lifted her off the ground.

She tried to scream, tried to break free, but it was as if she no longer had any control over her body. Her captor carried her into the woods as she fought to keep her eyes open. But the battle was soon lost.

* * * *

Shay startled awake, confused, her body aching. Her arms were numb and her head was almost too heavy to lift, but she forced herself to raise it. She was tied by ropes wrapped around her wrists and then fastened to stakes driven into a stone wall. Naked, she shivered at the chill in the air. Although she tugged as hard as she could, the bindings wouldn't give. Instead, the rough ropes dug into her skin and blood trickled down her arms. Her feet were free, but she had to stand on the tips of her toes to keep from straining at the ropes.

She squinted until, at last, her eyes adjusted to the dim light. A cavern spread out before her. Several campfires surrounded a larger one in the center of the cave. Around the fire sat twenty or thirty of The Cursed. She gasped as they turned their terrible, glittering red eyes toward her. Growls and snarls erupted as they jumped to their feet, dashing toward her only to stop and run back toward the fire.

Their leader stood, his long, skeletal-thin body stretching to a height a foot taller than those around him. His mouth opened wide, exposing his dagger-like fangs. His black tongue flicked out of his mouth and swiped over his upper lip. Knocking one of his pack away from him, he sauntered toward her.

The scream was on the tip of her tongue, but she wouldn't turn it free. Instead, she held her head high and met his gaze dead-on. At once, the cold allure that she'd felt at the pond swept over her and she forced her gaze away from his.

His pack followed him, the hungry expressions on their faces all too clear. As he grew closer, she picked up his awful scent. It burned her nostrils and drifted into her throat. Her throat closed and she found it hard to breathe.

He stopped only inches from her then leaned over to put his face even closer to hers. Again, the powerful pull of his eyes drew her in, and he threw back his head and laughed a dreadful sound. She kept her head up and hoped the fear stiffening her spine wouldn't show on her face as she struggled not to get lost in his dark orbs. He looked more alien than either werewolf or human.

His grin spread as he flicked out his tongue and slid it across her cheek. His touch broke the hold he had on her. She whipped her head to the side and tried to pull away, but he dug his long claws into her shoulders and held her. The coarse texture of his tongue was horrible, but it didn't compare to the foul stench of his breath. She was shaking by the time he turned her loose.

"Mine."

She dared to face him again. If he meant she was his, he was dead wrong. "Like hell I am."

Suddenly, she wished she could have one last minute with Rosh, Renkon, and Walker. If so, she'd tell them how much she loved them. She'd beg them to make her their mate and change her so that she'd be a werewolf like them.

Why did it take so long for me to realize what I really want? I belong to my men, Rosh, Walker, and Renkon, and no one else. She held back another sob, one that would've been filled with regret. *If only I had another chance. Now they'll never know that I choose them. Now and forever, I choose them.*

He clutched her breasts and squeezed. The evil glint in his eyes spoke volumes. Her scream erupted before she had a chance to keep it back. Cackling, he bent over and bit her breasts, bringing blood to redden her flesh. Driving his hand between her legs, he sunk his fingers into her pussy then yanked them out. Holding up his hand for all to see, he lashed out his tongue and licked her juices from his fingers. His pack roared their approval with howls and barks.

Turning to her, he took her by the chin then grabbed her hair and tore a hunk from her head. She gritted her teeth, keeping another scream inside.

His eyes blazed with lust. "Mine."

Spinning around, he jumped, flying through the air to land next to the fire. Holding up her hair in his fist, he flung it into the flames. The strands of her hair sizzled and sent sparks floating upward.

As if on cue, the pack sat back on their haunches, lifted their heads, and howled.

* * * *

Rosh led the others into the woods. He hadn't let himself think about what may have happened to Shay until now. Right after Myla had rushed into the camp shouting for help, he'd gathered a group of shifters and had headed toward the lake.

"If he's hurt her, I want first crack at him."

"Get in line, Walker. Rosh is going to tear out his heart while I rip his guts apart." Renkon's face hardened into a mask of fury

"You're wrong. He has no heart to rip out." Rosh put his left hand on his cousin's shoulder then thrust out his right to Walker.

Walker locked on to his arm, placing their forearms together in The Hidden's handshake of brotherhood. "We'll get her back, Rosh. I swear I'll give my last breath to do it."

"We'll do it as a team, the three of us. And once this is over, we make her our mate. Agreed?" They'd already made their peace the night Shay had stayed with Renkon, but what they had to do today would only enhance their bond. Their love for Shay and their need to keep her safe was all that mattered.

"Agreed. Let's do this."

The three of them led the way, moving as fast as they could toward the lake. Others joined them, eager to back up their brothers. Even Myla, refusing to stay behind while her friend was in danger, joined the group.

She hurried alongside Rosh, trying to keep pace with his long stride. "I can't help but blame myself. If I hadn't jumped into the pond without her, maybe they wouldn't have had the chance to take her."

Rosh kept moving. "It's not your fault. Shay wouldn't want you to think that. Besides, Burac would've found another way. We should've stopped him before now."

"Perhaps. But that's not our way."

He knew she was right. The people of The Hidden preferred peace over conflict. "I know, but there are times when peace has to be set aside. Saving Shay is one of those times."

He picked up a scent as they approached the lake. "Here. I can smell him here."

Rosh drew in more of the putrid aroma and snarled. Burac hadn't bothered to cover his scent. It didn't matter if that was because of a mistake or out of cockiness. Either way, Rosh was determined to rid the world of Burac.

"Let's get him."

Rosh nodded at Walker. They shifted, shedding their clothes and dropping to all fours. Snarling, they waited as the others shifted into their animal forms. With Rosh in the lead, they bounded into the forest and headed toward the caves of The Cursed.

* * * *

Shay prayed that Myla was safe. She hadn't seen any sign of her in the cave, and since the little shifter had gone into the water, she hoped that Burac hadn't seen her. Surely, Myla would know something had gone wrong since Shay's clothes were still on the ground. Had Myla made it back and spread the word of her abduction? Was help on the way?

She wasn't sure how long she stayed tied to the wall, but she wiggled her legs and flexed her hands, trying to take away the numbness. If she got a chance to escape, she had to be ready to take it.

Would Rosh, Renkon, and Walker come after her once they'd figured out what had happened? Would they know where to look?

She closed her eyes and pictured her men. And they were her men. She'd been afraid of committing to them, and yet, with the possibility of a life with them being taken away, she realized that she'd already pledged herself to them in her heart. Her mind had been slower to accept it, but now she was sure. If she lived to return to them, she'd make them her mates as fast as she could.

Why did I waste so much time? How stupid could I be? She opened her eyes to the terrible scene in front of her. *Please, God, let me survive and go home to my men. I want to spend the rest of my days in The Hidden, raising their children and making them happy. Please, please.*

The Cursed danced around the fire for the next hour, eating raw meat and squabbling. Fights broke out over food and drink while the males shared the females. Their sex held no trace of love but was brutal and animalistic. Men struck the women, who were forced to get on their hands and knees and open their asses to them. The women weren't much better as they abused their young ones, beating them with the bones of other animals. Shay watched in horror and tried not to think of what they intended to do to her.

At last, Burac shouted a strange and guttural sound and raised his fist into the air. At once, the rest of them stopped whatever they were doing and bowed in front of him. He surveyed his pack like a king surveying his subjects.

Facing her, he spoke the word she'd come to dread. "Mine."

She feared her heart would stop when he started toward her. She cringed to look at him, but his evil expression was nothing compared to his long, ugly dick. The sight of it brought bile to her mouth. He was going to rape her, and she could do nothing to stop him.

Chapter Ten

"No!"

Burac ignored her cry as he used a machete-style knife to shred the bindings around her wrists. She tried to strike out, but she couldn't get her numb arms to work. He took her by the hair, digging into her scalp, sending agonizing stabs of pain into her head, and yanked her along with him toward the fire.

The pack let out growls and snarls but kept their distance as Burac flung her to the hard stone floor then raised the knife into the air. She bit down on her tongue, and blood flooded her mouth.

"Mine."

She pushed onto her hands and knees then twisted around to glare at him. "Go fuck yourself."

His malicious grin opened to expose his fangs. She tried not to think of them sinking into her neck. Getting behind her, he pushed her forward until she fell onto her forearms. She jolted as his paw-like hand flattened against her butt cheek with a resounding *thwack*. But she didn't cry out. As long as she had a breath in her body, she'd fight him. He cackled as he bent over her, his cock in his hand.

She craned her head around to send him a sultry look. "Do you want some of this, asshole?"

His gaze fell to her ass as she wiggled it enticingly. The pack's frenzy grew louder. He tilted his head at her, and she cringed at the lustful glint in his eyes.

"You do, don't you?" She wiggled some more. "Then here it is."

Putting as much strength as she could into it, she kicked back much like a mule would. Luck was with her as her heel connected with his crotch. He let out a yowl and stumbled backward. She scrambled away, crawling before she managed to get to her feet. But with the pack surrounding them, she had nowhere to run.

She took a breath, ready to confront him, and swore she'd do the best she could. Her only regret would be that she'd never see the people of The Hidden or Renkon, Rosh, and Walker again. A vision of their life together that would never happen flashed across her mind, hurting more than anything Burac could ever do to her.

Silently, she sent a message to them. *I'm so sorry. I love you. Even if you never get to hear me say the words, I hope somehow, some way you'll know how much I cared.*

Burac, saliva dripping from the corners of his mouth, fury making his hideous face even uglier, stalked toward her, the machete in his fist. She took a couple of deep breaths, shouted a battle cry, then launched her body at him.

She surprised him and hit him hard, taking the bony body backward with her momentum. But he was stronger and flipped her on her back. He held her down, pinning her arms above her head as two of his pack held her legs down. He dropped the knife and shoved his dick between her legs. Terror filled her as she vainly struggled. Closing her eyes, she whispered a farewell message to the men she loved.

I love you. All of you.

An uproar had her opening her eyes as Burac jumped away from her. She lifted onto her elbows and gaped at the sight.

Werewolves, werebears, and other were-animals poured through the cave's opening. A huge white polar bear lumbered into the cave on their heels and headed straight for her.

They're here! With Myla!

Burac let out a screech then wrapped his hand around her throat and forced her to her knees.

Growls, snarls echoed around the chamber as fangs and claws slashed out. Blood flew as limbs and fur separated from bodies. Some of The Cursed managed to flee, but the shifters caught many of them.

Their mighty jaws clamped down on the enemies' throats to shake them until they were limp.

Renkon, Rosh, and Walker battled to get closer to her, but the pack closed ranks around the three werewolves, keeping them from getting to Shay. Although her fingernails were no match for Burac's claws, she dug them into his scrawny leg. He snarled, saliva falling from his jaws as he twisted around to strike her across the face.

She fell to the floor and the world spun around her. A terrifying growl came seconds before a bloodcurdling scream. She blinked, trying to get her eyes to focus as Myla the polar bear lifted onto her hind legs. Her huge mouth opened as she roared at Burac, and her white fangs shone in the firelight. Pulling back one enormous leg, she prepared to lash out at the smaller Burac.

But neither Myla nor Shay saw Burac snatch up the long knife in time to stop him. Shay reached out to Myla, her cry lost in Burac's howl, as he drove the blade deep into the bear's chest. Myla howled an angry, frustrated sound then knocked him away. She fell onto all fours, blood spurting from the wound in her chest.

"Myla!"

Myla turned to face her, and she could see her friend in the animal's face. A second later, four of The Cursed jumped on Myla's back, their claws digging into her body, their fangs biting her. Blood spewed outward, darkening her beautiful white fur as Myla roared and fought to throw them off. But she was no match for the beasts.

Shay staggered to her feet, determined to save her friend. She threw her body at the creatures and they jumped away, but it was too late. Myla slumped to the floor. She fell beside her, no longer seeing anything except her dying friend.

"No. Myla, please. No." Shay clung to her friend's still form as tears streamed down her face.

For one blissful moment, she thought she felt Myla move. She leaned back, hoping to see her friend open her eyes. Instead, her body blurred until Myla's naked human form lay next to her.

"Noooo." Her cry turned into moans of grief.

"Mine."

Fury flooded her. She lifted her head and turned to see Burac standing near her. The battle raged on around them, but her sole focus was on him.

"You're going to pay for this."

His horrid cackle made her stomach flip over. Pushing away from the floor, her hand came to rest beside Myla's leg that was farthest away from Burac, and she felt the sticky edge of the knife against her fingers. Moving as little as possible, she closed her hand around the hilt.

"Don't come near me."

As she'd hoped, he lurched closer, putting his body only a foot from her. He bent over, opened his jaws wide, and flexed his claws.

"Mine."

She looked into the face of evil and smiled. "Go to hell."

As fast and as hard as she could, she lunged upward and sunk the knife into his throat. Blood spurted onto her hand, her arm, her face and body, but she barely noticed. Burac tried to scream, but the sound came out in strangled gurgles. She let her smile grow bigger and pushed the blade in deeper, harder. His eyes bulged as he reached for her.

She twisted the knife and sneered. "Die, motherfucker."

The life in his eyes faded, and his arms fell limp. She pushed him away, letting the knife stay stuck in his throat. Shuddering, she fell to the floor.

* * * *

Shay hugged Kira to her. A week had passed in a strange state of activity interspersed with periods of waiting that had left her reflective.

The Hidden had lost some of its own in the fight with The Cursed. Two werewolves as well as a werecat and Myla had given their lives to save her. Burac had bruised and scratched her, but she'd never taken ill. Penn thought she was immune to The Cursed's venom and would, hopefully, pass her immunity along to her children. But thoughts of children would have to come later.

At first, she'd thought that the others would blame her for the deaths of their loved ones. If she hadn't come to their home, those precious lives wouldn't have been lost. Or if she'd chosen to mate with Rosh, Renkon, and Walker earlier, maybe Burac wouldn't have taken her and the conflict would've been avoided. But the people of The Hidden had welcomed her back into their lives, telling her that she wasn't at fault. To blame her would be like cursing the sun for letting the moon rise. What was meant to happen had happened, and no one was to bear any guilt.

She sat outside the huge new hut the men had built. They'd treated her with tenderness and concern, giving her the time she'd needed to mourn for her friend and the others. She'd cried wrapped in Rosh's arms at The Mourning Ceremony then had stilled her own tears to let Kira cling to her as she wept for her mother.

"They're ready for you." Rosh, looking strong and sexy in a white cotton shirt and pair of jeans, offered his hand to her. She took it, keeping Kira's in her own.

"Let's do this."

Rosh led them into the cabin where The Council as well as many others, including Renkon and Walker, waited. Charlton sat at a table along with Xnax, Tina, and the werecat Wisa. The werewolf Dagon who had sat on The Council was one of those lost in the battle, and another council member had yet to be selected.

Charlton tipped his head in greeting. "Shay Mathews, we are happy to see that you are well."

"Thank you. But I wish I could trade places with those who came to my rescue."

Xnax shook his head. "It was their choice, and The Time for Mourning has passed. We need to move on to other matters. We've given you more than enough time to make a decision."

This is it. Although she'd already told the men that she wanted to become their mate and stay, she hadn't made an official announcement. She drew her body straighter. "I want to stay." She hadn't expected any cheers, but she'd hoped for some kind of a reaction.

"And will you change?" Xnax bounced a sphere of fire from hand to hand. "Are you prepared to become werewolf?"

She'd thought about it a long time and had spoken to other werewolf females. Parts of it, like the pain that came with the transformation, made her nervous. Yet other aspects of it were thrilling. She longed to run through the forest, to see into the darkness, and to feel the tug of the moon. But even if being a werewolf was the worst thing in the world, she was still ready to face it. She wanted to be like her mates, and changing would bring them even closer.

"You don't have to become a werewolf," added Charlton. "But no one has ever mated in The Hidden and not changed."

"I want to and I will. Tonight, if possible."

"You must also choose mates in order to stay." Tina's silver eyes twinkled with delight. Everyone knew the men wanted her and that she wanted them. The only thing left was for Shay to publicly choose them.

"Then I choose Rosh, Renkon, and Walker."

Charlton shifted his gaze to the men, who'd gathered behind her. "Is this what you three want?"

"We do." They spoke in unison, and their powerful voices sent a shiver of desire through her.

"But there's another I'd like to choose."

Murmurs broke out around her. Charlton recovered from his surprise and asked, "Who else would you choose?"

"I don't want another mate. But I do want to choose Kira to be my adopted daughter. If that's what she wants."

All eyes fell on the young girl who clutched her hand. She squirmed under the attention.

"Is this what you want, Kira? Remember, your mother has family on The Outside. If you like, we could take you to them." Charlton's tone was soft and tender.

Kira shook her head. "I don't want to leave The Hidden. I want to stay with Shay and her men. My mother would've liked that."

He gazed past Shay and Kira. "What do you three say? Will you accept the responsibility of caring for Kira?"

She turned around to see her men nod. Walker spoke for all of them. "We'd like that very much."

Charlton looked to the other council members for their agreement. "Then consider Shay your adoptive mother."

Kira and Shay hugged each other then let go so that Kira could move to join the crowd. Shay turned back to The Council. "I'd like to request one more thing."

Tina laughed a bell-like sound. "It seems you'd like a lot of things. But go ahead. Ask."

"I'd like to have The Pledging Ceremony as soon as possible."

Tina threw out her arms and grinned as the crowd around her applauded. "It's about time you asked, Shay Mathews. It's about time."

* * * *

Shay stepped forward to stand under the ancient tree where she'd seen Bisna and her mates pledge their love and devotion. Walker stood across from her while Rosh and Renkon bumped shoulders, vying like boys squabbling in the schoolyard, to get the closest to her. They were sexy as hell in their cotton slacks and bare chests. Rosh had swept his hair away from his forehead while a lock of Renkon's fell across his forehead. Walker's dark gaze fixed on her, warming her with unspoken passion.

A breeze blew the fragrance of the surrounding flowers to her, and she drank in the aroma, committing it to memory. Every sight, sound, and scent of the day would live on inside her for the rest of her life.

She was barefoot, and her thin white dress flowed around her ankles. Although Kira and the other children weren't allowed at the ceremony, the young girl had combed her hair, intertwining yellow daisies in the strands. In remembrance of her mother, she'd added Myla's favorite blue ribbon to a lock of Shay's hair. Shay lifted her head to see the sunlight filtering through the branches of the huge tree as the birds gave voice to their gifts of song.

Charlton emerged from the crowd and took his place in front of them. His long blue robe flowed around him, making him appear even more regal and commanding than he always did. He cleared his throat, pressed his palms together, and the talking around them ceased.

"Shay Mathews, do you pledge to honor the men you've chosen? Will you lie with them at night, keeping their bodies warm and their hearts filled with your love? Will you treasure them as they vow to treasure you? Will you give them a life complete with pleasure and happiness? Will you keep them safe as they will keep you free from harm?"

She shifted her attention from Charlton to her men. "I pledge to do these things and more." Without shyness, she untied the knot in the top of her dress and let the soft material fall to the ground. She kept her attention on her men's faces and hoped they could see the love in her eyes.

Charlton faced the men. "Do you, Rosh, Walker, and Renkon, pledge to honor the woman who has chosen you? Will you give her your bodies each night, keeping her warm and her heart filled with your love? Will you treasure her as she vows to treasure you? Will you give her a life complete with pleasure and happiness? And will you keep her safe as she will keep you free from harm?"

Rosh winked at her and joined his friend and cousin in answering. "I pledge to do these things and more."

Together, her gorgeous, loving men dropped their slacks to the ground. Her pulse picked up speed. In only a short time, she'd take them to their new bed in the huge hut they'd made and show them just how much she loved them.

Charlton lifted his hands over their heads as they stepped closer together. "People of The Hidden, do you accept this union? Do you pledge to honor them as they live and grow together?"

Her new friends raised their voices as one. "We do!"

Shay held out both her hands. "Okay, guys, let's go home." She laughed as Rosh and Walker took her hands, leaving Renkon to take her arm. "Easy, boys, there's enough of me to go around."

* * * *

Shay stepped into her new home. Although she'd already spent the past week in the new hut, she still couldn't believe that she'd finally found the home for her. She'd traveled to many places, all lacking in comparison to her hometown of Passion, Colorado, but she'd always sensed an empty part of her. Only when she'd come to The Hidden and found the men who she'd chosen as her mates had the hole in her heart been filled.

The hut was much larger than their previous one. They'd even gone so far as to put in wooden floors and pane-less windows with shutters they could close at night. Two rooms—one for Kira and the other she'd share with her men—lay on either side of the common living quarters with its pallets for guests and the open fire pit in the middle. Candles cast soft shadows on the walls while the petals of various flowers, their colors forming a rainbow on the floor, led to the bedroom.

The place was a shack compared to the luxurious mansion she'd grown up in, but to her eyes, it was the most beautiful place in the world. As she'd learned from her men and others, supernatural beings didn't need the comforts of modern living. Instead, they preferred to live close to nature and spend as much time as they could in their alternate forms. They'd only stayed human for so long in deference to her.

She peeked into the bedroom and saw how the men had laid out blankets all over the floor. Tears came to her eyes as she thought of the many happy years that lay ahead with the men who loved her. They came up behind her, not touching her but giving her time to take it all in.

"This is so amazing."

"Are you sure it's okay? We could go to The Outside soon and take you to one of those fancy hotels where they have fine linen and hot water." Rosh trailed a finger down her back to the crack of her bottom.

"And room service," added Renkon. "I wouldn't mind having room service."

She faced them so they could not only hear the truth but see it on her face. "No way. I couldn't ask for a better place. I'm home with the men I love, and that's all I need. Damn, I love you all so much."

Walker gave her the biggest smile she'd ever seen. "You finally said it."

"Said what?"

"You finally said that you love us."

She scoffed as she tried to remember. "Naw. I've said it before. Lots of times. I'm positive of it."

"You've pledged your love and you've told us that you care for us, but you've never said those exact words."

She searched Rosh's face then the other two men's. "I'm sorry. I didn't realize."

"It doesn't matter now." Walker took a look toward Kira's room. "She's at Tina's, right?"

"She is. I'm sure she's probably knee-deep in fairy dust by now." She dropped her gaze to take in their erect cocks. "We're all alone, so why don't we make the best of it?"

"Good." Rosh picked her up and slung her over his shoulder.

She yelped then reached out to Walker and Renkon for help. "What the hell are you doing? Help me, you two."

But the other men ignored her as Rosh strode into the room then plopped her down on the pads of blankets. The three of them stood over her, their chests like mountains she wanted to climb.

"You're our woman."

She made a funny face. "Yeah. I think that's what The Pledging Ceremony was all about. But do me a favor, okay?"

"Anything," answered Renkon.

She licked her lips, eager to taste their cocks one by one. "Just don't ever say the word *mine*."

They didn't understand, but she didn't care. If she never heard that word again, she'd die a happy woman.

Walker fell to his knees. "Done."

She pulled him into her arms as he fell on top of her then rolled to her side. He pulled on one of her legs, spreading her wide for Rosh to see her pussy. She giggled and reached down to pull her folds apart.

"Do you like what you see?"

"Hell, yeah."

"Tell us what you see, Rosh." Renkon held his cock in his hand as he went to his knees beside her.

"She's beautiful. Her pussy is a pale pink like a perfect pearl. She's glistening with her juices." Rosh skimmed his finger around her clit then around her opening.

Renkon moaned and played with her breasts. She took Walker's hand and placed it on her other breast. She squirmed, enticing them to do more as the heat between her legs grew. Moaning a sound that changed into her imitation of a growl, she shot Rosh a look, urging him to stop teasing her.

He laughed then flicked his finger over her clit. She bucked and tried to move closer to him, but Walker and Renkon held her still.

Walker leaned over to give her a quick bite on her breast. "Should we change her first or after we fuck her?"

"You have to bite me to change me, right?" She frowned at a question she'd had before but hadn't asked. "Why is it that you can bite other things and they don't change into werewolves?"

"There are different bites for different things. Plus, we don't bite unless we mean to either kill or to change someone. Biting The Cursed had no effect on them since they already have werewolf blood in them." Rosh crouched down on his belly and slipped his hands under her bottom. "Enough talk. It's time for better things."

He put his face close to her pussy, and although she was ready for his move, she still jerked at his touch. He drew in her scent in a long sniff.

"Damn, but her scent is intoxicating. I love the way you smell."

"Then show me."

Rosh swept his tongue across her tender clit, making her jump again. His laughter was muffled as he pressed his mouth to her pussy and stuck his tongue inside.

"She's quick to the touch." Renkon pinched her nipples between his fingers. "See how her body responds?"

"I want to do more than just feel it." Walker dragged his tongue over her skin and up to her ear. He traced his tongue in circles around her sensitive skin, pausing twice to whisper how much he loved her.

Her body came alive under their touches, singing with every stroke they made, every word they said. She sensed their need grow as hers did. Walker and Renkon caressed her, their fingers roaming everywhere as they bent over her to explore her body with their mouths and tongues. She went to take their cocks in her hands, but they pushed them away, leaving her grasping at the blanket.

She closed her eyes then opened them. She'd felt their love before. Now she wanted them to dominate her. They could use the primal instinct she sensed inside them to take her as their woman, their lover, and their mate. "Don't hold back. I want you to love me, but I want to know you lust for me, too."

Rosh lifted his head to check with her. "Are you sure? It can get rough."

She licked her lips. "I'm sure. I know you'd never hurt me."

She could see the change in them, see the animallike glint in their eyes as sparks of red ignited in them. Tamping down the alarm that threatened to force its way into her, she refused to let what lay beneath their skin frighten her. Whether they were in their wolf forms or in their human bodies, they had put their lives on the line for her. She'd trust them to keep her safe. Yet she had another reason. She wanted to experience the tip of their beasts before she, too, welcomed her own wolf.

They were werewolves, and she was proud to call them her mates. "Hold her still."

Walker and Renkon held her legs down, binding her to the ground so that Rosh could devour her pussy. Still she bucked, unable to calm the fire flaming into an uncontrollable beast of its own. She cried out, not to get away but to let Rosh how much he pleased her.

Walker freed her leg to let Renkon take it. Moving so that he knelt beside her, he cupped her behind the head and gave his cock to her. "Suck on it as hard as you can. Do it."

She obeyed him, thrilling at the command in his tone. He was her master as surely as she was his queen. Licking and sucking on him, she did her best to take him as far into her mouth as she could. His fingers locked onto her hair, keeping her where she was even when she choked a little.

Renkon kept her legs apart as he bent over her to nibble on her stomach. His quick zings of pain added to the nips Rosh gave her clit. Rosh added fingers to her pussy, driving hard and fast into her. His hand rammed against the skin between her pussy and her butt hole, making loud smacking sounds that were an accompaniment to his sucking noises as he lapped up her juices.

Renkon turned her legs loose and shoved a hand under ass. "Tell us now what she looks like, Rosh." He played the tips of his fingers around the tight rings of her anus.

His cousin pulled back the hood of her clit and moaned a tortured yet satisfied sound. "I can feel her throbbing. Damn, she's ready to shoot."

"Then make her do it," added Walker.

Rosh didn't need any additional urging. He clamped on to her, making a circle with his mouth around her clit. He flicked his tongue over her little nub then sucked as he added a third finger to her pussy.

She trembled as the tension inside her grew. She didn't care if everyone in The Hidden heard her, she had to let go. She screamed Rosh's name, begging him to stop, growling at him if he dared to obey her. He continued to torment her until she was lifting her butt off the ground to imitate the way her body soared with the orgasm. She screamed again, and the sound morphed into moans of pleasure.

Walker hauled her body up, thrilling her as he positioned her on top of him. His hand covered her mons to hold her to him and to slide a finger between her folds to massage her clit.

"I'll drink your cream the next time. But for now, I can't wait any longer." Holding her from behind, he wrapped his arm around her breasts and pushed on her hip, thrusting his cock inside her pussy. He filled her completely.

She reached behind her to grab his hair as he placed bites along her neck. "Fuck me hard, Walker."

He answered, grunting as he plunged into her. Rosh and Renkon looked on, their cocks in their hands, the red flashes continuing in their eyes. She rode him, pushing her buttocks against him to ease the way for him. Bouncing her up and down, he pumped into her, harder with each thrust. A snarl formed on Rosh's face as he took her arms and pulled her away out of Walker's hold.

Walker's growl was low and mean, but Rosh wasn't going to be denied. "Easy, man. You've had her pussy, now take her ass."

He lay back, bending his legs so that he could lean backward between them. His cock stood straight up as he pulled her down on top of him. His enormous shaft stretched her to the limit and found her sweet spot.

The world erupted around her as she thrust forward, driving her climax into high gear. She leaned over Rosh, her hands shoved against his rock-hard chest as Walker smeared something cool and wet around her anus. He eased one finger inside her butt hole and worked it around, then two. He prepared her, but his preparation drove her crazy, too.

She tossed her hair over her back to turn and look at him. "Don't be so easy on me. I don't want gentle."

If he'd wanted to speak, she doubted he could have. Instead, he gritted his teeth, positioned the tip of his cock at her hole, and then pushed in.

She moaned at the pain, but the pain soon turned to pleasure. Pushing back, she worked her hips, moving them around as though to drill him farther inside her. Walker pulled the cheeks of her ass apart and plunged into her again and again. His tight balls slapped against her. He was filling her hole, and she loved it. She wondered how she could take two huge cocks inside her without tearing her body in half.

"Shay."

Renkon had risen to his feet. He held his cock and yanked her hair to bring her mouth to him. She tugged him in and deep-throated him.

Rosh closed his eyes, and she knew he was on the precipice of letting go. "Rosh, look at me."

He did, and as she'd expected, the sight of her licking Renkon's cock as she plumped her breasts between her arms sent him over the edge. He roared his release, shooting his seed into her.

Renkon kicked at his cousin's side. "Move, man. Get out of the way."

Rosh brought his legs up and rolled away, but not without first giving her breasts a quick squeeze. He grinned and came to his hands and feet. "Fuck her, Walker. Make her asshole as raw as her pussy's going to be."

She wanted to be raw. Wanted that fucked-good-and-hard feeling.

She drew in her cheeks to enclose her mouth around Renkon's cock. He was huge, soft yet hard with a musky taste she'd never tire of. Moaning, she hoped they would understand her meaning.

Walker ground into her, and she felt the warmth of his release flood into her hot, dark core. Slowing down his thrusts, he shoved into her, paused, then shoved again. She turned Renkon's cock loose to give Walker encouragement he really didn't need.

"Give it to me. I want every drop of you filling me."

He pulled out, stunning her until he positioned his cock at her asshole and rammed inside her again. He made a sound deep in his throat as he sent the last of his cum into her.

"Finally. You're"—Renkon slapped his hand over his mouth—"ready."

She laughed, but her laugh was lost in a shriek of surprise as Renkon picked her up and threw her into the air. She yelped, but that changed into a giggle as he caught her then fell with her to the blanket.

Rosh and Walker moved to the side, giving them more room. "The whole place must hear us," quipped Walker.

"Let them eat their hearts out."

Renkon was the only one who didn't laugh at her joke. His eyes were focused on her pussy as he yanked her closer and shoved his cock inside her. Putting his body over hers, he held her face between his hands and made her look at him.

He rocked against her, driving his cock as far as he could go. He was as large as the other two men and just as intense. He held her, his eyes firing with red flecks as he claimed her. But with each thrust, she claimed him in return.

A tear streaked down her cheek, but she wasn't sure he saw it. He was too intent on making her his own, and then, suddenly, he tensed a moment before his hot cum filled her. She held on to him and knew without a doubt that she'd finally found the place she would call home forever.

Renkon fell on top of her until the other two men pulled him off her. Her body tingled with satisfaction but also with something more than mere sexual release. She was overjoyed, happier than she'd ever been.

She reached out for them, determined to make the night even more memorable. "I want you to change me now."

They exchanged glances then nodded as they pulled her into an upright position. Rosh slid behind her to support her by leaning her back against his chest. Renkon massaged her foot and ran his palm along her leg. Walker took her arm.

"Are you really ready?"

She saw the concern in Renkon's eyes and wanted to wipe it away for good. "Yes."

"It's going to hurt, and you'll pass out. You'll sleep for a couple of days, but we'll watch over you, so don't worry." Rosh brushed her hair back from her ear.

"I'll never worry as long as you're all around."

"When you wake up, you'll change that same night." Walker kissed the palm of her hand. Gone was the beast, tamed by her love.

"I can't wait. So what else? Do I have to do anything?" Her heart pounded in her chest, but she was ready.

"Just remember how much we love you." Renkon bent over her leg and shifted, bringing out his fangs.

She let out a slow breath. "How could I ever forget?"

Renkon bit into her leg, searing pain up the limb and into her stomach. Rosh's fangs sunk into her neck just as Walker shifted, dropping his jaw as his fangs erupted from his gums, then plunged them into her arm.

The pain was sheer agony as it ripped inward, burning a trail toward her heart. She screamed a horrible, deafening sound as she slipped away into the darkness.

Epilogue

"I'm calling bullshit on both of you." Maya Switt gaped at them.

Shay laughed and shrugged at Tatum. She could understand Maya's disbelief. Who would've thought either one of them would've ended up living with three great men?

Shay crossed her heart. "I swear it's the truth. In fact, there they are."

The women looked out the window of Tony's Diner of Passion, Colorado, to find seven men standing on the street corner, talking and joking around. Rosh grinned at her and tilted his head, a gesture she'd come to learn most werewolves did whenever they had a question. She waved and felt, as she always did, the rush of lust sweep through her. Walker tapped Renkon on the shoulder, and they, too, gave her sexy grins. It had taken a lot of coaxing to get the men to come to Passion with her, but she was glad they had. She'd missed Tatum, and running into her old friend Maya had been a bonus.

"Okay, so I've met Tatum's guys, the Shelton brothers, but who's the other hunk? Please tell me he's not aiming to make a fourth for either of you." Maya plopped back against the booth, making her curly blonde hair bounce. "Three men for one woman is just not fair. I mean, come on. I've spent the past two years in New York City and haven't found even one good man. All the men I've met are too civilized. I want a man's man. Someone who has a wild side I can tame. Do you know the type of man I'm talking about?"

Shay smothered a laugh as Tatum widened her eyes at her. "Yeah, we know the type."

"So tell me. Who's the other guy?"

"That's a friend of Rosh's, James W. Hunter. And no, I have no plans to make him my fourth."

Tatum shook her head as she took another bite of her cheeseburger. "Uh-uh. Me, either. Three's enough."

"Good. So what's his story? What's he do?"

Shay paused, unsure of what to say. She couldn't tell her that he lived as a werewolf in The Hidden. Her new home was a closely guarded secret, and she hadn't even told Tatum. She'd revealed that she and her men were werewolves just as Tatum and her men were, but that was all. Tatum's life was on The Outside, so there was no reason to tell her.

"Uh, I'm not sure. But I do know that his two brothers are as hot as he is. Why don't I introduce you and you can find out all about him for yourself?"

Maya took the bait just as Shay had figured she would. "Yeah. Definitely. But let me freshen up first."

She bumped against Tatum's shoulder, who slid out of the booth to let her friend out. Giving James another once-over, Maya hurried toward the ladies' room at the back of the restaurant.

Tatum checked around her to see who might be listening then leaned over the table. "Should we tell her what he is?"

Shay slid her gaze over her men, who were striding toward the entrance of the diner. "Shoot no. Where's the fun in that?"

THE END

WWW.JANEJAMISON.COM

ABOUT THE AUTHOR

Jane Jamison has always liked "weird stuff" as her mother called it. From an early age she was fascinated with stories about werewolves, vampires, space, aliens, and whatever was hiding in her bedroom closet (to this day, she still swears she can hear growls and moans whenever the lights are out).

Being born under the sign of Scorpio meant Jane was destined to be very sensual. Some would say she was (and remains) downright sexual. Then one day she put her two favorite things together on paper and found her life's true ambition: to be an erotica paranormal romance author.

Jane spends at least six days a week locked in her office surrounded by the characters she loves. Every day a new character will knock on the door of her imagination. Her plans include taking care of her loving husband, traveling, and writing at least twelve books a year.

For all titles by Jane Jamison, please visit
www.bookstrand.com/jane-jamison

Siren Publishing, Inc.
www.SirenPublishing.com

Lightning Source UK Ltd.
Milton Keynes UK
UKOW04f1852130813

215323UK00016B/806/P